Margaret McKinnon

Class III

Portree. Sec School

Portree

Skye

· A ·
GOOD·BOOK
· IS · THE ·
PRECIOUS
LIFE-BLOOD
OF · A
MASTER
SPIRIT
—MILTON

PRINTED IN   GREAT BRITAIN

J. CONRAD

The KINGS TREASURIES
OF LITERATURE

GENERAL EDITOR
Sir A·T·QUILLER COUCH

LONDON : J·M·DENT & SONS LTD.

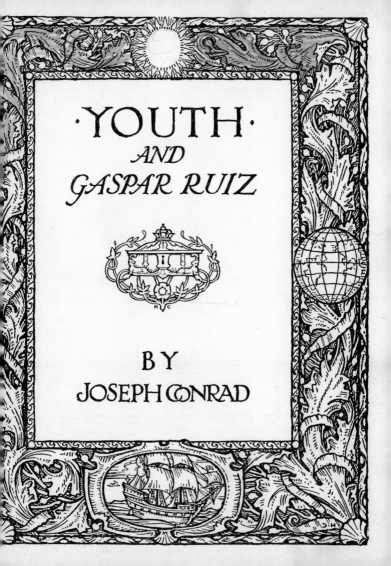

·YOUTH·
AND
GASPAR RUIZ

BY
JOSEPH CONRAD

CONTENTS

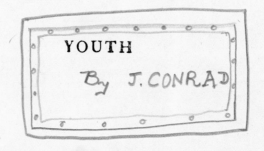

YOUTH

By J. CONRAD

YOUTH

THIS could have occurred nowhere but in England, where men and sea interpenetrate, so to speak—the sea entering into the life of most men, and the men knowing something or everything about the sea, in the way of amusement, of travel, or of bread-winning.

We were sitting round a mahogany table that reflected the bottle, the claret-glasses, and our faces as we leaned on our elbows. There was a director of companies, an accountant, a lawyer, Marlow, and myself. The director had been a *Conway* boy, the accountant had served four years at sea, the lawyer—a fine crusted Tory, High Churchman, the best of old fellows, the soul of honour—had been chief officer in the P. & O. service in the good old days when mail-boats were square-rigged at least on two masts, and used to come down the China Sea before a fair monsoon with stun'-sails set alow and aloft. We all began life in the merchant service. Between the five of us there was the strong bond of the sea, and also the fellowship of the craft, which no amount of enthusiasm for yachting, cruising, and

*
9

so on can give, since one is only the amusement
of life and the other is life itself.

Marlow (at least I think that is how he spelt
his name) told the story, or rather the chronicle,
of a voyage:—

" Yes, I have seen a little of the Eastern seas;
but what I remember best is my first voyage
there. You fellows know there are those voyages
that seem ordered for the illustration of life, that
might stand for a symbol of existence. You fight,
work, sweat, nearly kill yourself, sometimes do
kill yourself, trying to accomplish something—
and you can't. Not from any fault of yours. You
simply can do nothing, neither great nor little—
not a thing in the world—not even marry an old
maid, or get a wretched 600-ton cargo of coal to
its port of destination.

" It was altogether a memorable affair. It was
my first voyage to the East, and my first voyage
as second mate; it was also my skipper's first
command. You'll admit it was time. He was
sixty if a day; a little man, with a broad, not
very straight back, with bowed shoulders and one
leg more bandy than the other, he had that queer
twisted-about appearance you see so often in men
who work in the fields. He had a nut-cracker
face—chin and nose trying to come together over
a sunken mouth—and it was framed in iron-grey

fluffy hair, that looked like a chin-strap of cotton-wool sprinkled with coal-dust. And he had blue eyes in that old face of his, which were amazingly like a boy's, with that candid expression some quite common men preserve to the end of their days by a rare internal gift of simplicity of heart and rectitude of soul. What induced him to accept me was a wonder. I had come out of a crack Australian clipper, where I had been third officer, and he seemed to have a prejudice against crack clippers as aristocratic and high-toned. He said to me, 'You know, in this ship you will have to work.' I said I had to work in every ship I had ever been in. 'Ah, but this is different, and you gentlemen out of them big ships; . . . but there! I dare say you will do. Join to-morrow.'

"I joined to-morrow. It was twenty-two years ago; and I was just twenty. How time passes! It was one of the happiest days of my life. Fancy! Second mate for the first time—a really responsible officer! I wouldn't have thrown up my new billet for a fortune. The mate looked me over carefully. He was also an old chap, but of another stamp. He had a Roman nose, a snow-white, long beard, and his name was Mahon, but he insisted that it should be pronounced Mann. He was well connected; yet there was something wrong with his luck, and he had never got on.

" As to the captain, he had been for years in coasters, then in the Mediterranean, and last in the West Indian trade. He had never been round the Capes. He could just write a kind of sketchy hand, and didn't care for writing at all. Both were thorough good seamen of course, and between those two old chaps I felt like a small boy between two grandfathers.

" The ship also was old. Her name was the *Judea*. Queer name, isn't it? She belonged to a man Wilmer, Wilcox—some name like that; but he has been bankrupt and dead these twenty years or more, and his name don't matter. She had been laid up in Shadwell Basin for ever so long. You may imagine her state. She was all rust, dust, grime—soot aloft, dirt on deck. To me it was like coming out of a palace into a ruined cottage. She was about 400 tons, had a primitive windlass, wooden latches to the doors, not a bit of brass about her, and a big square stern. There was on it, below her name in big letters, a lot of scrollwork, with the gilt off, and some sort of a coat of arms, with the motto ' Do or Die ' underneath. I remember it took my fancy immensely. There was a touch of romance in it, something that made me love the old thing —something that appealed to my youth!

" We left London in ballast—sand ballast—

to load a cargo of coal in a northern port for
Bankok. Bankok! I thrilled. I had been six
years at sea, but had only seen Melbourne and
Sydney, very good places, charming places in
their way—but Bankok!

"We worked out of the Thames under canvas,
with a North Sea pilot on board. His name was
Jermyn, and he dodged all day long about the
galley drying his handkerchief before the stove.
Apparently he never slept. He was a dismal man,
with a perpetual tear sparkling at the end of his
nose, who either had been in trouble, or was in
trouble, or expected to be in trouble—couldn't
be happy unless something went wrong. He mis-
trusted my youth, my common-sense, and my
seamanship, and made a point of showing it in
a hundred little ways. I dare say he was right.
It seems to me I knew very little then, and I
know not much more now; but I cherish a hate
for that Jermyn to this day.

"We were a week working up as far as Yar-
mouth Roads, and then we got into a gale—the
famous October gale of twenty-two years ago. It
was wind, lightning, sleet, snow, and a terrific
sea. We were flying light, and you may imagine
how bad it was when I tell you we had smashed
bulwarks and a flooded deck. On the second
night she shifted her ballast into the lee bow, and

by that time we had been blown off somewhere
of the Dogger Bank. There was nothing for it
but go below with shovels and try to right her,
and there we were in that vast hold, gloomy like
a cavern, the tallow dips stuck and flickering on
the beams, the gale howling above, the ship
tossing about like mad on her side; there we all
were, Jermyn, the captain, every one, hardly
able to keep our feet, engaged on that grave-
digger's work, and trying to toss shovelfuls of
wet sand up to windward At every tumble of
the ship you could see vaguely in the dim light
men falling down with a great flourish of shovels
One of the ship's boys (we had two), impressed
by the weirdness of the scene, wept as if his heart
would break. We could hear him blubbering
somewhere in the shadows.

   " On the third day the gale died out, and by-
and-by a north-country tug picked us up. We
took sixteen days in all to get from London to
the Tyne! When we got into dock we had lost
our turn for loading, and they hauled us off to a
tier where we remained for a month. Mrs. Beard
(the captain's name was Beard) came from Col-
chester to see the old man. She lived on board.
The crew of runners had left, and there remained
only the officers, one boy, and the steward, a
mulatto who answered to the name of Abraham.

Mrs. Beard was an old woman, with a face all wrinkled and ruddy like a winter apple, and the figure of a young girl. She caught sight of me once, sewing on a button, and insisted on having my shirts to repair. This was something different from the captains' wives I had known on board crack clippers. When I brought her the shirts, she said: ' And the socks? They want mending, I am sure, and John's—Captain Beard's—things are all in order now. I would be glad of something to do.' Bless the old woman! She overhauled my outfit for me, and meantime I read for the first time *Sartor Resartus* and Burnaby's *Ride to Khiva*. I didn't understand much of the first then; but I remember I preferred the soldier to the philosopher at the time; a preference which life has only confirmed. One was a man, and the other was either more—or less. However, they are both dead, and Mrs. Beard is dead, and youth, strength, genius, thoughts, achievements, simple hearts—all dies. . . . No matter.

" They loaded us at last. We shipped a crew. Eight able seamen and two boys. We hauled off one evening to the buoys at the dock-gates, ready to go out, and with a fair prospect of beginning the voyage next day. Mrs. Beard was to start for home by a late train. When the ship was fast we went to tea. We sat rather silent through

the meal—Mahon, the old couple, and I. I
finished first, and slipped away for a smoke, my
cabin being in a deck-house just against the poop.
It was high water, blowing fresh with a drizzle;
the double dock-gates were opened, and the
steam-colliers were going in and out in the darkness with their lights burning bright, a great
plashing of propellers, rattling of winches, and
a lot of hailing on the pier-heads. I watched the
procession of head-lights gliding high and of
green lights gliding low in the night, when suddenly a red gleam flashed at me, vanished, came
into view again, and remained. The fore-end of
a steamer loomed up close. I shouted down the
cabin, ' Come up, quick! ' and then heard a
startled voice saying afar in the dark, ' Stop her,
sir.' A bell jingled. Another voice cried warn-
ingly, ' We are going right into that barque, sir.'
The answer to this was a gruff ' All right,' and
the next thing was a heavy crash as the steamer
struck a glancing blow with the bluff of her bow
about our fore-rigging. There was a moment of
confusion, yelling, and running about. Steam
roared. Then somebody was heard saying, ' All
clear, sir.' . . . ' Are you all right? ' asked the
gruff voice. I had jumped forward to see the
damage, and hailed back, ' I think so.' ' Easy
astern,' said the gruff voice. A bell jingled.

'What steamer is that?' screamed Mahon. By
that time she was no more to us than a bulky
shadow manœuvring a little way off. They
shouted at us some name—a woman's name,
Miranda or Melissa—or some such thing. 'This
means another month in this beastly hole,' said
Mahon to me, as we peered with lamps about the
splintered bulwarks and broken braces. 'But
where's the captain?'

"We had not heard or seen anything of him
all that time. We went aft to look. A doleful
voice arose hailing somewhere in the middle of
the dock, '*Judea* ahoy!' . . . How the devil
did he get there? . . . 'Hallo!' we shouted. 'I
am adrift in our boat without oars,' he cried. A
belated waterman offered his services, and Mahon
struck a bargain with him for half-a-crown to
tow our skipper alongside; but it was Mrs. Beard
that came up the ladder first. They had been
floating about the dock in that mizzly cold rain
for nearly an hour. I was never so surprised in
my life.

"It appears that when he heard my shout
'Come up' he understood at once what was the
matter, caught up his wife, ran on deck, and
across, and down into our boat, which was fast
to the ladder. Not bad for a sixty-year-old. Just
imagine that old fellow saving heroically in his

arms that old woman—the woman of his life.
He set her down on a thwart, and was ready to
climb back on board when the painter came
adrift somehow, and away they went together.
Of course in the confusion we did not hear him
shouting. He looked abashed. She said cheerfully, ' I suppose it does not matter my losing
the train now? ' ' No, Jenny—you go below and
get warm,' he growled. Then to us: ' A sailor
has no business with a wife—I say. There I was,
out of the ship. Well, no harm done this time.
Let's go and look at what that fool of a steamer
smashed.'

"It wasn't much, but it delayed us three
weeks. At the end of that time, the captain being
engaged with his agents, I carried Mrs. Beard's
bag to the railway-station and put her all comfy
into a third-class carriage. She lowered the
window to say, ' You are a good young man. If
you see John — Captain Beard — without his
muffler at night, just remind him from me to
keep his throat well wrapped up.' ' Certainly,
Mrs. Beard,' I said. ' You are a good young man;
I noticed how attentive you are to John—to Captain——' The train pulled out suddenly; I took
my cap off to the old woman: I never saw her
again. . . . Pass the bottle.

"We went to sea next day. When we made

that start for Bankok we had been already three
months out of London. We had expected to be a
fortnight or so—at the outside.

"It was January, and the weather was beautiful—the beautiful sunny winter weather that
has more charm than in the summer-time, because it is unexpected, and crisp, and you know
it won't, it can't, last long. It's like a wind-
fall, like a godsend, like an unexpected piece of
luck.

"It lasted all down the North Sea, all down
Channel; and it lasted till we were three hundred
miles or so to the westward of the Lizards: then
the wind went round to the sou'west and began
to pipe up. In two days it blew a gale. The
Judea, hove to, wallowed on the Atlantic like an
old candle-box. It blew day after day: it blew
with spite, without interval, without mercy,
without rest. The world was nothing but an immensity of great foaming waves rushing at us,
under a sky low enough to touch with the hand
and dirty like a smoked ceiling. In the stormy
space surrounding us there was as much flying
spray as air. Day after day and night after night
there was nothing round the ship but the howl
of the wind, the tumult of the sea, the noise of
water pouring over her deck. There was no rest
for her and no rest for us. She tossed, she pitched,

she stood on her head, she sat on her tail, she rolled, she groaned, and we had to hold on while on deck and cling to our bunks when below, in a constant effort of body and worry of mind.

" One night Mahon spoke through the small window of my berth. It opened right into my very bed, and I was lying there sleepless, in my boots, feeling as though I had not slept for years, and could not if I tried. He said excitedly—

" ' You got the sounding-rod in here, Marlow? I can't get the pumps to suck. By God! it's no child's play.'

" I gave him the sounding-rod and lay down again, trying to think of various things—but I thought only of the pumps. When I came on deck they were still at it, and my watch relieved at the pumps. By the light of the lantern brought on deck to examine the sounding-rod I caught a glimpse of their weary, serious faces. We pumped all the four hours. We pumped all night, all day, all the week—watch and watch. She was working herself loose, and leaked badly—not enough to drown us at once, but enough to kill us with the work at the pumps. And while we pumped the ship was going from us piecemeal: the bulwarks went, the stanchions were torn out, the ventilators smashed, the cabin-door burst in. There was not a dry spot in the ship. She was being

gutted bit by bit. The long-boat changed, as if
by magic, into matchwood, where she stood in
her gripes. I had lashed her myself, and was
rather proud of my handiwork, which had with-
stood so long the malice of the sea. And we
pumped. And there was no break in the weather.
The sea was white like a sheet of foam, like a
caldron of boiling milk; there was not a break
in the clouds, no—not the size of a man's hand—
no, not for so much as ten seconds. There was
for us no sky, there were for us no stars, no sun,
no universe—nothing but angry clouds and an
infuriated sea. We pumped watch and watch,
for dear life; and it seemed to last for months,
for years, for all eternity, as though we had been
dead and gone to a hell for sailors. We forgot the
day of the week, the name of the month, what
year it was, and whether we had ever been
ashore. The sails blew away, she lay broadside
on under a weather-cloth, the ocean poured over
her, and we did not care. We turned those
handles, and had the eyes of idiots. As soon as
we had crawled on deck I used to take a round
turn with a rope about the men, the pumps, and
the mainmast, and we turned, we turned incessantly, with the water to our waists, to our necks,
over our heads. It was all one. We had forgotten
how it felt to be dry.

" And there was somewhere in me the thought: By Jove! this is the deuce of an adventure— something you read about; and it is my first voyage as second mate—and I am only twenty —and here I am lasting it out as well as any of these men, and keeping my chaps up to the mark. I was pleased. I would not have given up the experience for worlds. I had moments of exultation. Whenever the old dismantled craft pitched heavily with her counter high in the air, she seemed to me to throw up, like an appeal, like a defiance, like a cry to the clouds without mercy, the words written on her stern: ' *Judea*, London. Do or Die.'

" O youth! The strength of it, the faith of it, the imagination of it! To me she was not an old rattle-trap carting about the world a lot of coal for a freight—to me she was the endeavour, the test, the trial of life. I think of her with pleasure, with affection, with regret—as you would think of some one dead you have loved. I shall never forget her. . . . Pass the bottle.

" One night when tied to the mast, as I explained, we were pumping on, deafened with the wind, and without spirit enough in us to wish ourselves dead, a heavy sea crashed aboard and swept clean over us. As soon as I got my breath I shouted, as in duty bound, ' Keep on, boys! '

when suddenly I felt something hard floating on deck strike the calf of my leg. I made a grab at it and missed. It was so dark we could not see each other's faces within a foot—you understand.

"After that thump the ship kept quiet for a while, and the thing, whatever it was, struck my leg again. This time I caught it—and it was a saucepan. At first, being stupid with fatigue and thinking of nothing but the pumps, I did not understand what I had in my hand. Suddenly it dawned upon me, and I shouted, 'Boys, the house on deck is gone. Leave this, and let's look for the cook.'

"There was a deck-house forward, which contained the galley, the cook's berth, and the quarters of the crew. As we had expected for days to see it swept away, the hands had been ordered to sleep in the cabin—the only safe place in the ship. The steward, Abraham, however, persisted in clinging to his berth, stupidly, like a mule—from sheer fright I believe, like an animal that won't leave a stable falling in an earthquake. So we went to look for him. It was chancing death, since once out of our lashings we were as exposed as if on a raft. But we went. The house was shattered as if a shell had exploded inside. Most of it had gone overboard—stove, men's quarters, and their property, all was gone; but

two posts, holding a portion of the bulkhead to
which Abraham's bunk was attached, remained
as if by a miracle. We groped in the ruins and
came upon this, and there he was, sitting in his
bunk, surrounded by foam and wreckage, jab-
bering cheerfully to himself. He was out of his
mind; completely and for ever mad, with this
sudden shock coming upon the fag-end of his
endurance. We snatched him up, lugged him
aft, and pitched him head-first down the cabin
companion. You understand there was no time
to carry him down with infinite precautions and
wait to see how he got on. Those below would
pick him up at the bottom of the stairs all right.
We were in a hurry to go back to the pumps.
That business could not wait. A bad leak is an
inhuman thing.

"One would think that the sole purpose of that
fiendish gale had been to make a lunatic of that
poor devil of a mulatto. It eased before morning,
and next day the sky cleared, and as the sea went
down the leak took up. When it came to bending
a fresh set of sails the crew demanded to put
back—and really there was nothing else to do.
Boats gone, decks swept clean, cabin gutted, men
without a stitch but what they stood in, stores
spoiled, ship strained. We put her head for home,
and—would you believe it? The wind came east

right in our teeth. It blew fresh, it blew continuously. We had to beat up every inch of the way,
but she did not leak so badly, the water keeping
comparatively smooth. Two hours' pumping in
every four is no joke—but it kept her afloat as
far as Falmouth.

"The good people there live on casualties of
the sea, and no doubt were glad to see us. A
hungry crowd of shipwrights sharpened their
chisels at the sight of that carcass of a ship. And,
by Jove! they had pretty pickings off us before
they were done. I fancy the owner was already
in a tight place. There were delays. Then it was
decided to take part of the cargo out and caulk
her topsides. This was done, the repairs finished,
cargo reshipped; a new crew came on board, and
we went out—for Bankok. At the end of a week
we were back again. The crew said they weren't
going to Bankok—a hundred and fifty days'
passage—in a something hooker that wanted
pumping eight hours out of the twenty-four;
and the nautical papers inserted again the little
paragraph: ' *Judea*. Barque. Tyne to Bankok;
coals; put back to Falmouth leaky and with
crew refusing duty.'

"There were more delays—more tinkering.
The owner came down for a day, and said she was
as right as a little fiddle. Poor old Captain Beard

looked like the ghost of a Geordie skipper—
through the worry and humiliation of it. Remember he was sixty, and it was his first command. Mahon said it was a foolish business, and
would end badly. I loved the ship more than
ever, and wanted awfully to get to Bankok. To
Bankok! Magic name, blessed name. Mesopo-
tamia wasn't a patch on it. Remember I was
twenty, and it was my first second-mate's billet,
and the East was waiting for me.

" We went out and anchored in the outer roads
with a fresh crew—the third. She leaked worse
than ever. It was as if those confounded shipwrights had actually made a hole in her. This
time we did not even go outside. The crew simply
refused to man the windlass.

" They towed us back to the inner harbour,
and we became a fixture, a feature, an institution
of the place. People pointed us out to visitors
as ' That 'ere barque that's going to Bankok—
has been here six months—put back three times.'
On holidays the small boys pulling about in boats
would hail, ' *Judea*, ahoy! ' and if a head showed
above the rail shouted, ' Where you bound to?—
Bankok? ' and jeered. We were only three on
board. The poor old skipper mooned in the cabin.
Mahon undertook the cooking, and unexpectedly
developed all a Frenchman's genius for preparing

nice little messes. I looked languidly after the
rigging. We became citizens of Falmouth. Every
shopkeeper knew us. At the barber's or tobacco-
nist's they asked familiarly, ' Do you think you
will ever get to Bankok? ' Meantime the owner,
the underwriters, and the charterers squabbled
amongst themselves in London, and our pay went
on. . . . Pass the bottle.

" It was horrid. Morally it was worse than
pumping for life. It seemed as though we had
been forgotten by the world, belonged to nobody,
would get nowhere; it seemed that, as if bewitched, we would have to live for ever and ever
in that inner harbour, a derision and a byword
to generations of long-shore loafers and dishonest
boatmen. I obtained three months' pay and a
five days' leave, and made a rush for London.
It took me a day to get there and pretty well
another to come back—but three months' pay
went all the same. I don't know what I did with
it. I went to a music-hall, I believe, lunched,
dined, and supped in a swell place in Regent
Street, and was back to time, with nothing but
a complete set of Byron's works and a new rail-
way rug to show for three months' work. The
boatman who pulled me off to the ship said:
' Hallo! I thought you had left the old thing.
She will never get to Bankok.' ' That's all *you*

know about it,' I said scornfully—but I didn't
like that prophecy at all.

" Suddenly a man, some kind of agent to somebody, appeared with full powers. He had grog-
blossoms all over his face, an indomitable energy,
and was a jolly soul. We leaped into life again.
A hulk came alongside, took our cargo, and then
we went into dry dock to get our copper stripped.
No wonder she leaked. The poor thing, strained
beyond endurance by the gale, had, as if in disgust, spat out all the oakum of her lower seams.
She was recaulked, new coppered, and made as
tight as a bottle. We went back to the hulk and
reshipped our cargo.

" Then, on a fine moonlight night, all the rats
left the ship.

" We had been infested with them. They had
destroyed our sails, consumed more stores than
the crew, affably shared our beds and our dangers,
and now, when the ship was made seaworthy,
concluded to clear out. I called Mahon to enjoy
the spectacle. Rat after rat appeared on our rail,
took a last look over his shoulder, and leaped with
a hollow thud into the empty hulk. We tried to
count them, but soon lost the tale. Mahon said:
' Well, well! don't talk to me about the intelligence of rats. They ought to have left before,
when we had that narrow squeak from founder-

ing. There you have the proof how silly is the superstition about them. They leave a good ship for an old rotten hulk, where there is nothing to eat, too, the fools! . . . I don't believe they know what is safe or what is good for them, any more than you or I.'

" And after some more talk we agreed that the wisdom of rats had been grossly overrated, being in fact no greater than that of men.

" The story of the ship was known, by this, all up the Channel from Land's End to the Forelands, and we could get no crew on the south coast. They sent us one all complete from Liverpool, and we left once more—for Bankok.

" We had fair breezes, smooth water right into the tropics, and the old *Judea* lumbered along in the sunshine. When she went eight knots everything cracked aloft, and we tied our caps to our heads; but mostly she strolled on at the rate of three miles an hour. What could you expect? She was tired—that old ship. Her youth was where mine is—where yours is—you fellows who listen to this yarn; and what friend would throw your years and your weariness in your face? We didn't grumble at her. To us aft, at least, it seemed as though we had been born in her, reared in her, had lived in her for ages, had never known any other ship. I would just as soon have abused the old village church at home for not being a cathedral.

" And for me there was also my youth to make me patient. There was all the East before me, and all life, and the thought that I had been tried in that ship and had come out pretty well. And I thought of men of old who, centuries ago, went that road in ships that sailed no better, to the land of palms, and spices, and yellow sands, and of brown nations ruled by kings more cruel than Nero the Roman and more splendid than Solomon the Jew. The old bark lumbered on, heavy with her age and the burden of her cargo, while I lived the life of youth in ignorance and hope. She lumbered on through an interminable procession of days; and the fresh gilding flashed back at the setting sun, seemed to cry out over the darkening sea the words painted on her stern, '*Judea*, London. Do or Die.'

" Then we entered the Indian Ocean and steered northerly for Java Head. The winds were light. Weeks slipped by. She crawled on, do or die, and people at home began to think of posting us as overdue.

" One Saturday evening, I being off duty, the men asked me to give them an extra bucket of water or so—for washing clothes. As I did not wish to screw on the fresh-water pump so late,

I went forward whistling, and with a key in my hand to unlock the forepeak scuttle, intending to serve the water out of a spare tank we kept there.

" The smell down below was as unexpected as it was frightful. One would have thought hundreds of paraffin-lamps had been flaring and smoking in that hole for days. I was glad to get out. The man with me coughed and said, ' Funny smell, sir.' I answered negligently, ' It's good for the health, they say,' and walked aft.

" The first thing I did was to put my head down the square of the midship ventilator. As I lifted the lid a visible breath, something like a thin fog, a puff of faint haze, rose from the opening. The ascending air was hot, and had a heavy, sooty, paraffiny smell. I gave one sniff, and put down the lid gently. It was no use choking myself. The cargo was on fire.

" Next day she began to smoke in earnest. You see it was to be expected, for though the coal was of a safe kind, that cargo had been so handled, so broken up with handling, that it looked more like smithy coal than anything else. Then it had been wetted—more than once. It rained all the time we were taking it back from the hulk, and now with this long passage it got heated, and there was another case of spontaneous combustion.

"The captain called us into the cabin. He had a chart spread on the table, and looked unhappy. He said, 'The coast of West Australia is near, but I mean to proceed to our destination. It is the hurricane month too; but we will just keep her head for Bankok, and fight the fire. No more putting back anywhere, if we all get roasted. We will try first to stifle this 'ere damned combustion by want of air.'

"We tried. We battened down everything, and still she smoked. The smoke kept coming out through imperceptible crevices; it forced itself through bulkheads and covers; it oozed here and there and everywhere in slender threads, in an invisible film, in an incomprehensible manner. It made its way into the cabin, into the forecastle; it poisoned the sheltered places on the deck, it could be sniffed as high as the mainyard. It was clear that if the smoke came out the air came in. This was disheartening. This combustion refused to be stifled.

"We resolved to try water, and took the hatches off. Enormous volumes of smoke, whitish, yellowish, thick, greasy, misty, choking, ascended as high as the trucks. All hands cleared out aft. Then the poisonous cloud blew away, and we went back to work in a smoke that was no thicker now than that of an ordinary factory chimney.

" We rigged the force-pump, got the hose along, and by-and-by it burst. Well, it was as old as the ship—a prehistoric hose, and past repair. Then we pumped with the feeble head-pump, drew water with buckets, and in this way managed in time to pour lots of Indian Ocean into the main hatch. The bright stream flashed in sunshine, fell into a layer of white crawling smoke, and vanished on the black surface of coal. Steam ascended mingling with the smoke. We poured salt water as into a barrel without a bottom. It was our fate to pump in that ship, to pump out of her, to pump into her; and after keeping water out of her to save ourselves from being drowned, we frantically poured water into her to save ourselves from being burnt.

" And she crawled on, do or die, in the serene weather. The sky was a miracle of purity, a miracle of azure. The sea was polished, was blue, was pellucid, was sparkling like a precious stone, extending on all sides, all round to the horizon—as if the whole terrestrial globe had been one jewel, one colossal sapphire, a single gem fashioned into a planet. And on the lustre of the great calm waters the *Judea* glided im-

B

perceptibly, enveloped in languid and unclean vapours, in a lazy cloud that drifted to leeward, light and slow: a pestiferous cloud defiling the splendour of sea and sky.

"All this time of course we saw no fire. The cargo smouldered at the bottom somewhere. Once Mahon, as we were working side by side, said to me with a queer smile: 'Now, if she only would spring a tidy leak—like that time when we first left the Channel—it would put a stopper on this fire. Wouldn't it?' I remarked irrelevantly, 'Do you remember the rats?'

"We fought the fire and sailed the ship too as carefully as though nothing had been the matter. The steward cooked and attended on us. Of the other twelve men, eight worked while four rested. Every one took his turn, captain included. There was equality, and if not exactly fraternity, then a deal of good feeling. Sometimes a man, as he dashed a bucketful of water down the hatchway, would yell out, 'Hurrah for Bankok!' and the rest laughed. But generally we were taciturn and serious—and thirsty. Oh! how thirsty! And we had to be careful with the water. Strict allowance. The ship smoked, the sun blazed. . . . Pass the bottle.

"We tried everything. We even made an attempt to dig down to the fire. No good, of course. No man could remain more than a minute below. Mahon, who went first, fainted there, and the man who went to fetch him out did likewise. We lugged them out on deck. Then I leaped down to show how easily it could be done. They had learned wisdom by that time, and contented themselves by fishing for me with a chain-hook tied to a broom-handle, I believe. I did not offer to go and fetch up my shovel, which was left down below.

" Things began to look bad. We put the long-boat into the water. The second boat was ready to swing out. We had also another, a 14-foot thing, on davits aft, where it was quite safe.

" Then, behold, the smoke suddenly decreased. We redoubled our efforts to flood the bottom of the ship. In two days there was no smoke at all. Everybody was on the broad grin. This was on a Friday. On Saturday no work, but sailing the ship of course, was done. The men washed their clothes and their faces for the first time in a fortnight, and had a special dinner given them. They spoke of spontaneous combustion with contempt, and implied *they* were the boys to put out combustions. Somehow we all felt as though we each had inherited a large fortune. But a beastly smell of burning hung about the ship. Captain Beard had hollow eyes and sunken cheeks. I had

never noticed so much before how twisted and
bowed he was. He and Mahon prowled soberly
about hatches and ventilators, sniffing. It struck
me suddenly poor Mahon was a very, very old
chap. As to me, I was as pleased and proud as
though I had helped to win a great naval battle.
O! Youth!

"The night was fine. In the morning a home-
ward-bound ship passed us hull down—the first
we had seen for months; but we were nearing
the land at last, Java Head being about 190 miles
off, and nearly due north.

"Next day it was my watch on deck from
eight to twelve. At breakfast the captain observed, 'It's wonderful how that smell hangs
about the cabin.' About ten, the mate being on
the poop, I stepped down on the main-deck for
a moment. The carpenter's bench stood abaft
the mainmast: I leaned against it sucking at my
pipe, and the carpenter, a young chap, came to
talk to me. He remarked, 'I think we have done
very well, haven't we?' and then I perceived
with annoyance the fool was trying to tilt the
bench. I said curtly, 'Don't, Chips,' and immediately became aware of a queer sensation, of
an absurd delusion,—I seemed somehow to be in
the air. I heard all round me like a pent-up
breath released—as if a thousand giants simul-

taneously had said Phoo!—and felt a dull con-
cussion which made my ribs ache suddenly. No
doubt about it—I was in the air, and my body
was describing a short parabola. But short as it
was, I had the time to think several thoughts in,
as far as I can remember, the following order:
' This can't be the carpenter—What is it?—Some
accident—Submarine volcano?—Coals, gas!—By
Jove! we are being blown up—Everybody's dead
—I am falling into the after-hatch—I see fire
in it.'

" The coal-dust suspended in the air of the hold
had glowed dull-red at the moment of the explosion. In the twinkling of an eye, in an infini-
tesimal fraction of a second since the first tilt of
the bench, I was sprawling full length on the
cargo. I picked myself up and scrambled out. It
was quick like a rebound. The deck was a wilderness of smashed timber, lying crosswise like trees
in a wood after a hurricane; an immense curtain
of soiled rags waved gently before me—it was
the mainsail blown to strips. I thought, The
masts will be toppling over directly; and to get
out of the way bolted on all-fours towards the
poop-ladder. The first person I saw was Mahon,
with eyes like saucers, his mouth open, and the
long white hair standing straight on end round
his head like a silver halo. He was just about to

go down when the sight of the main-deck stirring, heaving up, and changing into splinters before his eyes, petrified him on the top step. I stared at him in unbelief, and he stared at me with a queer kind of shocked curiosity. I did not know that I had no hair, no eyebrows, no eyelashes, that my young moustache was burnt off, that my face was black, one cheek laid open, my nose cut, and my chin bleeding. I had lost my cap, one of my slippers, and my shirt was torn to rags. Of all this I was not aware. I was amazed to see the ship still afloat, the poop-deck whole—and, most of all, to see anybody alive. Also the peace of the sky and the serenity of the sea were distinctly surprising. I suppose I expected to see them convulsed with horror. . . . Pass the bottle.

" There was a voice hailing the ship from some-where—in the air, in the sky—I couldn't tell. Presently I saw the captain—and he was mad. He asked me eagerly, ' Where's the cabin-table? ' and to hear such a question was a frightful shock. I had just been blown up, you understand, and vibrated with that experience,—I wasn't quite sure whether I was alive. Mahon began to stamp with both feet and yelled at him, ' Good God! don't you see the deck's blown out of her? ' I found my voice, and stammered out as if conscious of some gross neglect of duty, 'I don't know where the cabin-table is.' It was like an absurd dream.

"Do you know what he wanted next? Well, he wanted to trim the yards. Very placidly, and as if lost in thought, he insisted on having the foreyard squared. 'I don't know if there's anybody alive,' said Mahon, almost tearfully. 'Surely,' he said, gently, 'there will be enough left to square the foreyard.'

"The old chap, it seems, was in his own berth, winding up the chronometers, when the shock sent him spinning. Immediately it occurred to him—as he said afterwards—that the ship had struck something, and he ran out into the cabin. There, he saw, the cabin-table had vanished somewhere. The deck being blown up, it had fallen down into the lazarette, of course. Where we had our breakfast that morning he saw only a great hole in the floor. This appeared to him so awfully mysterious, and impressed him so immensely, that what he saw and heard after he got on deck were mere trifles in comparison. And, mark, he noticed directly the wheel deserted and his barque off her course—and his only thought was to get that miserable, stripped, undecked, smouldering shell of a ship back again with her head pointing at her port of destination. Bankok!

That's what he was after. I tell you this quiet,
bowed, bandy-legged, almost deformed little man
was immense in the singleness of his idea and in
his placid ignorance of our agitation. He motioned us forward with a commanding gesture,
and went to take the wheel himself.

"Yes; that was the first thing we did—trim
the yards of that wreck! No one was killed, or
even disabled, but every one was more or less
hurt. You should have seen them! Some were
in rags, with black faces, like coalheavers, like
sweeps, and had bullet heads that seemed closely
cropped, but were in fact singed to the skin.
Others, of the watch below, awakened by being
shot out from their collapsing bunks, shivered
incessantly, and kept on groaning even as we
went about our work. But they all worked. That
crew of Liverpool hard cases had in them the
right stuff. It's my experience they always have.
It is the sea that gives it—the vastness, the loneliness surrounding their dark stolid souls. Ah!
Well! we stumbled, we crept, we fell, we barked
our shins on the wreckage, we hauled. The
masts stood, but we did not know how much
they might be charred down below. It was
nearly calm, but a long swell ran from the west
and made her roll. They might go at any
moment. We looked at them with apprehen-

sion. One could not foresee which way they would
fall.

"Then we retreated aft and looked about us.
The deck was a tangle of planks on edge, of
planks on end, of splinters, of ruined woodwork.
The masts rose from that chaos like big trees
above a matted undergrowth. The interstices of
that mass of wreckage were full of something
whitish, sluggish, stirring—of something that was
like a greasy fog. The smoke of the invisible fire
was coming up again, was trailing, like a poisonous thick mist in some valley choked with dead
wood. Already lazy wisps were beginning to curl
upwards amongst the mass of splinters. Here
and there a piece of timber, stuck upright, resembled a post. Half of a fife-rail had been shot
through the foresail, and the sky made a patch of
glorious blue in the ignobly soiled canvas. A
portion of several boards holding together had
fallen across the rail, and one end protruded overboard, like a gangway leading upon nothing, like
a gangway leading over the deep sea, leading to
death—as if inviting us to walk the plank at
once and be done with our ridiculous troubles.
And still the air, the sky—a ghost, something
invisible was hailing the ship.

"Some one had the sense to look over, and
there was the helmsman, who had impulsively

*B

jumped overboard, anxious to come back. He
yelled and swam lustily like a merman, keeping
up with the ship. We threw him a rope, and presently he stood amongst us streaming with water
and very crestfallen. The captain had surrendered the wheel, and apart, elbow on rail and
chin in hand, gazed at the sea wistfully. We
asked ourselves, What next? I thought, Now,
this is something like. This is great. I wonder
what will happen. O youth!

"Suddenly Mahon sighted a steamer far
astern. Captain Beard said, 'We may do something with her yet.' We hoisted two flags, which
said in the international language of the sea, 'On
fire. Want immediate assistance.' The steamer
grew bigger rapidly, and by-and-by spoke with
two flags on her foremast, 'I am coming to your
assistance.'

" In half an hour she was abreast, to windward,
within hail, and rolling slightly, with her engines
stopped. We lost our composure, and yelled all
together with excitement, 'We've been blown
up.' A man in a white helmet, on the bridge,
cried, 'Yes! All right! all right!' and he nodded
his head, and smiled, and made soothing motions
with his hand as though at a lot of frightened
children. One of the boats dropped in the water,
and walked towards us upon the sea with her

long oars.   Four Calashes pulled a swinging
stroke. This was my first sight of Malay seamen.
I've known them since, but what struck me then
was their unconcern: they came alongside, and
even the bowman standing up and holding to
our main-chains with the boat-hook did not
deign to lift his head for a glance. I thought
people who had been blown up deserved more
attention.

" A little man, dry like a chip and agile like a
monkey, clambered up. It was the mate of the
steamer. He gave one look, and cried, ' O boys
—you had better quit.'

" We were silent. He talked apart with the
captain for a time,—seemed to argue with him.
Then they went away together to the steamer.

" When our skipper came back we learned that
the steamer was the *Sommerville*, Captain Nash,
from West Australia to Singapore *viâ* Batavia
with mails, and that the agreement was she
should tow us to Anjer or Batavia, if possible,
where we could extinguish the fire by scuttling,
and then proceed on our voyage—to Bankok!
The old man seemed excited. ' We will do it yet,'
he said to Mahon, fiercely. He shook his fist at
the sky. Nobody else said a word.

" At noon the steamer began to tow. She went
ahead slim and high, and what was left of the

Judea followed at the end of seventy fathom of tow-rope,—followed her swiftly like a cloud of smoke with mastheads protruding above. We went aloft to furl the sails. We coughed on the yards, and were careful about the bunts. Do you see the lot of us there, putting a neat furl on the sails of that ship doomed to arrive nowhere? There was not a man who didn't think that at any moment the masts would topple over. From aloft we could not see the ship for smoke, and they worked carefully, passing the gaskets with even turns. 'Harbour furl—aloft there!' cried Mahon from below.

"You understand this? I don't think one of those chaps expected to get down in the usual way. When we did I heard them saying to each other, 'Well, I thought we would come down overboard, in a lump—sticks and all—blame me if I didn't.' 'That's what I was thinking to myself,' would answer wearily another battered and bandaged scarecrow. And, mind, these were men without the drilled-in habit of obedience. To an onlooker they would be a lot of profane scallywags without a redeeming point. What made them do it—what made them obey me when I, thinking consciously how fine it was, made them drop the bunt of the foresail twice to try and do it better? What? They had no professional

reputation—no examples, no praise. It wasn't a
sense of duty; they all knew well enough how to
shirk, and laze, and dodge—when they had a
mind to it—and mostly they had. Was it the
two pounds ten a month that sent them there?
They didn't think their pay half good enough.
No; it was something in them, something inborn
and subtle and everlasting. I don't say positively
that the crew of a French or German merchant-
man wouldn't have done it, but I doubt whether
it would have been done in the same way. There
was a completeness in it, something solid like a
principle, and masterful like an instinct—a dis-
closure of something secret—of that hidden something, that gift of good or evil that makes racial
difference, that shapes the fate of nations.

" It was that night at ten that, for the first
time since we had been fighting it, we saw the
fire. The speed of the towing had fanned the
smouldering destruction. A blue gleam appeared
forward, shining below the wreck of the deck. It
wavered in patches, it seemed to stir and creep
like the light of a glowworm. I saw it first, and
told Mahon. ' Then the game's up,' he said.
' We had better stop this towing, or she will
burst out suddenly fore and aft before we can
clear out.' We set up a yell; rang bells to attract
their attention; they towed on. At last Mahon

and I had to crawl forward and cut the rope with an axe. There was no time to cast off the lashings. Red tongues could be seen licking the wilderness of splinters under our feet as we made our way back to the poop.

" Of course they very soon found out in the steamer that the rope was gone. She gave a loud blast of her whistle, her lights were seen sweeping in a wide circle, she came up ranging close alongside, and stopped. We were all in a tight group on the poop looking at her. Every man had saved a little bundle or a bag. Suddenly a conical flame with a twisted top shot up forward and threw upon the black sea a circle of light, with the two vessels side by side and heaving gently in its centre. Captain Beard had been sitting on the gratings still and mute for hours, but now he rose slowly and advanced in front of us, to the mizzen-shrouds. Captain Nash hailed: ' Come along! Look sharp. I have mail-bags on board. I will take you and your boats to Singapore.'

" ' Thank you! No! ' said our skipper. ' We must see the last of the ship.'

" ' I can't stand by any longer,' shouted the other. ' Mails—you know.'

" ' Ay! ay! We are all right.'

" ' Very well! I'll report you in Singapore. . . . Good-bye! '

" He waved his hand. Our men dropped their bundles quietly. The steamer moved ahead, and passing out of the circle of light, vanished at once from our sight, dazzled by the fire which burned fiercely. And then I knew that I would see the East first as commander of a small boat. I thought it fine; and the fidelity to the old ship was fine. We should see the last of her. Oh, the glamour of youth! Oh, the fire of it, more dazzling than the flames of the burning ship, throwing a magic light on the wide earth, leaping audaciously to the sky, presently to be quenched by time, more cruel, more pitiless, more bitter than the sea—and, like the flames of the burning ship, surrounded by an impenetrable night.

* * * * *

" The old man warned us in his gentle and inflexible way that it was part of our duty to save for the underwriters as much as we could of the ship's gear. Accordingly we went to work aft, while she blazed forward to give us plenty of light. We lugged out a lot of rubbish. What didn't we save? An old barometer fixed with an absurd quantity of screws nearly cost me my life: a sudden rush of smoke came upon me, and I just got away in time. There were various

stores, bolts of canvas, coils of rope; the poop
looked like a marine bazaar, and the boats were
lumbered to the gunwales. One would have
thought the old man wanted to take as much
as he could of his first command with him. He
was very, very quiet, but off his balance evi-
dently. Would you believe it? He wanted to take
a length of old stream-cable and a kedge-anchor
with him in the long-boat. We said, ' Ay, ay,
sir,' deferentially, and on the quiet let the things
slip overboard. The heavy medicine-chest went
that way, two bags of green coffee, tins of paint
—fancy, paint!—a whole lot of things. Then I
was ordered with two hands into the boats to
make a stowage and get them ready against the
time it would be proper for us to leave the ship.

" We put everything straight, stepped the long-
boat's mast for our skipper, who was to take
charge of her, and I was not sorry to sit down
for a moment. My face felt raw, every limb
ached as if broken, I was aware of all my ribs,
and would have sworn to a twist in the back-
bone. The boats, fast astern, lay in a deep
shadow, and all around I could see the circle of
the sea lighted by the fire. A gigantic flame
arose forward straight and clear. It flared fierce,
with noises like the whirr of wings, with rumbles
as of thunder. There were cracks, detonations,

and from the cone of flame the sparks flew upwards, as man is born to trouble, to leaky ships,
and to ships that burn.

" What bothered me was, that the ship lying
broadside to the swell and to such wind as
there was—a mere breath—the boats would not
keep astern where they were safe, but persisted,
in a pig-headed way boats have, in getting under
the counter and then swinging alongside. They
were knocking about dangerously and coming
near the flame, while the ship rolled on them,
and, of course, there was always the danger of
the masts going over the side at any moment.
I and my two boat-keepers kept them off as
best we could, with oars and boat-hooks; but
to be constantly at it became exasperating, since
there was no reason why we should not leave at
once. We could not see those on board, nor
could we imagine what caused the delay. The
boat-keepers were swearing feebly, and I had not
only my share of the work but also had to keep
at it two men who showed a constant inclination
to lay themselves down and let things slide.

" At last I hailed, ' On deck there,' and some
one looked over. ' We're ready here,' I said.
The head disappeared, and very soon popped up
again. ' The captain says, All right, sir, and to
keep the boats well clear of the ship.'

" Half an hour passed. Suddenly there was a frightful racket, rattle, clanking of chain, hiss of water, and millions of sparks flew up into the shivering column of smoke that stood leaning slightly above the ship. The cat-heads had burned away, and the two red-hot anchors had gone to the bottom, tearing out after them two hundred fathom of red-hot chain. The ship trembled, the mass of flame swayed as if ready to collapse, and the fore top-gallant-mast fell. It darted down like an arrow of fire, shot under, and instantly leaping up within an oar's-length of the boats, floated quietly, very black on the luminous sea. I hailed the deck again. After some time a man in an unexpectedly cheerful but also muffled tone, as though he had been trying to speak with his mouth shut, informed me, ' Coming directly, sir,' and vanished. For a long time I heard nothing but the whirr and roar of the fire. There were also whistling sounds. The boats jumped, tugged at the painters, ran at each other playfully, knocked their sides together, or, do what we would, swung in a bunch against the ship's side. I couldn't stand it any longer, and swarming up a rope, clambered aboard over the stern.

" It was as bright as day. Coming up like this, the sheet of fire facing me was a terrifying

sight, and the heat seemed hardly bearable at
first. On a settee cushion dragged out of the
cabin, Captain Beard, his legs drawn up and one
arm under his head, slept with the light playing
on him. Do you know what the rest were busy
about? They were sitting on deck right aft,
round an open case, eating bread and cheese and
drinking bottled stout.

" On the background of flames twisting in
fierce tongues above their heads they seemed at
home like salamanders, and looked like a band
of desperate pirates. The fire sparkled in the
whites of their eyes, gleamed on patches of white
skin seen through the torn shirts. Each had the
marks as of a battle about him—bandaged heads,
tied-up arms, a strip of dirty rag round a knee—
and each man had a bottle between his legs and
a chunk of cheese in his hand. Mahon got up.
With his handsome and disreputable head, his
hooked profile, his long white beard, and with
an uncorked bottle in his hand, he resembled one
of those reckless sea-robbers of old making merry
amidst violence and disaster. ' The last meal on
board,' he explained solemnly. ' We had nothing
to eat all day, and it was no use leaving all
this.' He flourished the bottle and indicated the
sleeping skipper. ' He said he couldn't swallow
anything, so I got him to lie down,' he went on;

and as I stared, ' I don't know whether you are
aware, young fellow, the man had no sleep to
speak of for days—and there will be dam' little
sleep in the boats.' ' There will be no boats by-
and-by if you fool about much longer,' I said,
indignantly. I walked up to the skipper and
shook him by the shoulder. At last he opened
his eyes, but did not move. ' Time to leave her,
sir,' I said, quietly.

"He got up painfully, looked at the flames, at
the sea sparkling round the ship, and black,
black as ink farther away; he looked at the
stars shining dim through a thin veil of smoke
in a sky black, black as Erebus.

"' Youngest first,' he said.

"And the ordinary seaman, wiping his mouth
with the back of his hand, got up, clambered
over the taffrail, and vanished. Others followed.
One, on the point of going over, stopped short
to drain his bottle, and with a great swing of
his arm flung it at the fire. ' Take this ! ' he
cried.

"The skipper lingered disconsolately, and we
left him to commune alone for a while with his
first command. Then I went up again and
brought him away at last. It was time. The
ironwork on the poop was hot to the touch.

"Then the painter of the long-boat was cut,

and the three boats, tied together, drifted clear
of the ship. It was just sixteen hours after the
explosion when we abandoned her. Mahon had
charge of the second boat, and I had the smallest
—the 14-foot thing. The long-boat would have
taken the lot of us; but the skipper said we
must save as much property as we could—for
the underwriters—and so I got my first command.
I had two men with me, a bag of biscuits, a few
tins of meat, and a breaker of water. I was
ordered to keep close to the long-boat, that in
case of bad weather we might be taken into
her.

"And do you know what I thought? I thought
I would part company as soon as I could. I
wanted to have my first command all to myself.
I wasn't going to sail in a squadron if there was
a chance for independent cruising. I would make
land by myself. I would beat the other boats.
Youth! All youth! The silly, charming, beautiful youth.

"But we did not make a start at once. We
must see the last of the ship. And so the boats
drifted about that night, heaving and setting
on the swell. The men dozed, waked, sighed,
groaned. I looked at the burning ship.

"Between the darkness of earth and heaven
she was burning fiercely upon a disc of purple

sea shot by the blood-red play of gleams; upon
a disc of water, glittering and sinister. A high,
clear flame, an immense and lonely flame, ascended from the ocean, and from its summit the
black smoke poured continuously at the sky. She
burned furiously; mournful and imposing like
a funeral pile kindled in the night, surrounded
by the sea, watched over by the stars. A magnificent death had come like a grace, like a gift,
like a reward to that old ship at the end of her
laborious days. The surrender of her weary
ghost to the keeping of stars and sea was stirring like the sight of a glorious triumph. The
masts fell just before daybreak, and for a moment
there was a burst and turmoil of sparks that
seemed to fill with flying fire the night patient
and watchful, the vast night lying silent upon
the sea. At daylight she was only a charred
shell, floating still under a cloud of smoke and
bearing a glowing mass of coal within.

" Then the oars were got out, and the boats
forming in a line moved round her remains as if
in procession—the long-boat leading. As we
pulled across her stern a slim dart of fire shot
out viciously at us, and suddenly she went down,
head first, in a great hiss of steam. The un-
consumed stern was the last to sink; but the
paint had gone, had cracked, had peeled off, and

there were no letters, there was no word, no
stubborn device that was like her soul, to flash
at the rising sun her creed and her name.

"We made our way north. A breeze sprang
up, and about noon all the boats came together
for the last time. I had no mast or sail in mine,
but I made a mast out of a spare oar and hoisted
a boat-awning for a sail, with a boat-hook for a
yard. She was certainly over-masted, but I had
the satisfaction of knowing that with the wind
aft I could beat the other two. I had to wait
for them. Then we all had a look at the captain's
chart, and, after a sociable meal of hard bread
and water, got our last instructions. These were
simple: steer north, and keep together as much
as possible. 'Be careful with that jury-rig,
Marlow,' said the captain; and Mahon, as I
sailed proudly past his boat, wrinkled his curved
nose and hailed, ' You will sail that ship of yours
under water, if you don't look out, young fellow.'
He was a malicious old man—and may the deep
sea where he sleeps now rock him gently, rock
him tenderly to the end of time!

" Before sunset a thick rain-squall passed over
the two boats, which were far astern, and that
was the last I saw of them for a time. Next day
I sat steering my cockle-shell—my first command
—with nothing but water and sky around me. I

did sight in the afternoon the upper sails of a
ship far away, but said nothing, and my men did
not notice her. You see I was afraid she might be
homeward bound, and I had no mind to turn
back from the portals of the East. I was steering
for Java—another blessed name—like Bankok,
you know. I steered many days.

"I need not tell you what it is to be knocking
about in an open boat. I remember nights and
days of calm, when we pulled, we pulled, and the
boat seemed to stand still, as if bewitched within
the circle of the sea horizon. I remember the
heat, the deluge of rain-squalls that kept us baling
for dear life (but filled our water-cask), and I remember sixteen hours on end with a mouth dry
as a cinder and a steering-oar over the stern to
keep my first command head on to a breaking
sea. I did not know how good a man I was till
then. I remember the drawn faces, the dejected
figures of my two men, and I remember my
youth and the feeling that will never come back
any more—the feeling that I could last for ever,
outlast the sea, the earth, and all men; the de-
ceitful feeling that lures us on to joys, to perils,
to love, to vain effort—to death; the triumphant
conviction of strength, the heat of life in the
handful of dust, the glow in the heart that with
every year grows dim, grows cold, grows small,

and expires—and expires, too soon, too soon—before life itself.

"And this is how I see the East. I have seen its secret places and have looked into its very soul; but now I see it always from a small boat, a high outline of mountains, blue and afar in the morning; like faint mist at noon; a jagged wall of purple at sunset. I have the feel of the oar in my hand, the vision of a scorching blue sea in my eyes. And I see a bay, a wide bay, smooth as glass and polished like ice, shimmering in the dark. A red light burns far off upon the gloom of the land, and the night is soft and warm. We drag at the oars with aching arms, and suddenly a puff of wind, a puff faint and tepid and laden with strange odours of blossoms, of aromatic wood, comes out of the still night—the first sigh of the East on my face. That I can never forget. It was impalpable and enslaving, like a charm, like a whispered promise of mysterious delight.

"We had been pulling this finishing spell for eleven hours. Two pulled, and he whose turn it was to rest sat at the tiller. We had made out the red light in that bay and steered for it, guessing it must mark some small coasting port. We passed two vessels, outlandish and high-sterned, sleeping at anchor, and, approaching the light, now very dim, ran the boat's nose against the end of a jutting wharf. We were blind with fatigue. My men dropped the oars and fell off the thwarts as if dead. I made fast to a pile. A current rippled softly. The scented obscurity of the shore was grouped into vast masses, a density of colossal clumps of vegetation, probably—mute and fantastic shapes. And at their foot the semi-circle of a beach gleamed faintly, like an illusion. There was not a light, not a stir, not a sound. The mysterious East faced me, perfumed like a flower, silent like death, dark like a grave.

"And I sat weary beyond expression, exulting like a conqueror, sleepless and entranced as if before a profound, a fateful enigma.

"A splashing of oars, a measured dip reverberating on the level of water, intensified by the silence of the shore into loud claps, made me jump up. A boat, a European boat, was coming in. I invoked the name of the dead; I hailed: *Judea* ahoy! A thin shout answered.

"It was the captain, I had beaten the flag-ship by three hours, and I was glad to hear the old man's voice again, tremulous and tired. 'Is it you, Marlow?' 'Mind the end of that jetty, sir,' I cried.

"He approached cautiously, and brought up with the deep-sea lead-line which we had saved—for the underwriters. I eased my painter and fell alongside. He sat, a broken figure at the stern, wet with dew, his hands clasped in his lap. His men were asleep already. ' I had a terrible time of it,' he murmured. ' Mahon is behind—not very far.' We conversed in whispers, in low whispers, as if afraid to wake up the land. Guns, thunder, earthquakes would not have awakened the men just then.

" Looking round as we talked, I saw away at sea a bright light travelling in the night. ' There's a steamer passing the bay,' I said. She was not passing, she was entering, and she even came close and anchored. ' I wish,' said the old man, ' you would find out whether she is English. Perhaps they could give us a passage somewhere.' He seemed nervously anxious. So by dint of punching and kicking I started one of my men into a state of somnambulism, and giving him an oar, took another and pulled towards the lights of the steamer.

" There was a murmur of voices in her, metal-lic hollow clangs of the engine-room, footsteps on the deck. Her ports shone, round like dilated eyes. Shapes moved about, and there was a shadowy man high up on the bridge. He heard my oars.

" And then, before I could open my lips, the East spoke to me, but it was in a Western voice.

A torrent of words was poured into the enigmatical, the fateful silence; outlandish, angry words, mixed with words and even whole sentences of good English, less strange but even more surprising. The voice swore and cursed violently; it riddled the solemn peace of the bay by a volley of abuse. It began by calling me Pig, and from that went crescendo into unmentionable adjectives—in English. The man up there raged aloud in two languages, and with a sincerity in his fury that almost convinced me I had, in some way, sinned against the harmony of the universe. I could hardly see him, but began to think he would work himself into a fit.

"Suddenly he ceased, and I could hear him snorting and blowing like a porpoise. I said—

"'What steamer is this, pray?'

"'Eh? What's this? And who are you?'

"'Castaway crew of an English barque burnt at sea. We came here to-night. I am the second mate. The captain is in the long-boat, and wishes to know if you would give us a passage somewhere.'

"'Oh, my goodness! I say. . . . This is the *Celestial* from Singapore on her return trip. I'll arrange with your captain in the morning, . . and, . . . I say, . . . did you hear me just now?'

" ' I should think the whole bay heard you.'

" ' I thought you were a shore-boat. Now, look here—this infernal lazy scoundrel of a care-taker has gone to sleep again—curse him. The light is out, and I nearly ran foul of the end of this damned jetty. This is the third time he plays me this trick. Now, I ask you, can anybody stand this kind of thing? It's enough to drive a man out of his mind. I'll report him. . . . I'll get the Assistant Resident to give him the sack, by . . . I See—there's no light. It's out, isn't it? I take you to witness the light's out. There should be a light, you know. A red light on the——'

" ' There was a light,' I said, mildly.

" ' But it's out, man! What's the use of talking like this? You can see for yourself it's out—don't you? If you had to take a valuable steamer along this God-forsaken coast you would want a light too. I'll kick him from end to end of his miserable wharf. You'll see if I don't. I will——'

" ' So I may tell my captain you'll take us? ' I broke in.

" ' Yes, I'll take you. Good night,' he said, brusquely.

" I pulled back, made fast again to the jetty, and then went to sleep at last. I had faced the

silence of the East. I had heard some of its
language. But when I opened my eyes again the
silence was as complete as though it had never
been broken. I was lying in a flood of light, and
the sky had never looked so far, so high, before.
I opened my eyes and lay without moving.

"And then I saw the men of the East—they
were looking at me. The whole length of the
jetty was full of people. I saw brown, bronze,
yellow faces, the black eyes, the glitter, the
colour of an Eastern crowd. And all these beings
stared without a murmur, without a sigh, without
a movement. They stared down at the boats, at
the sleeping men who at night had come to them
from the sea. Nothing moved. The fronds of
palms stood still against the sky. Not a branch
stirred along the shore, and the brown roofs of
hidden houses peeped through the green foliage,
through the big leaves that hung shining and
still like leaves forged of heavy metal. This was
the East of the ancient navigators, so old, so mysterious, resplendent and sombre, living and unchanged, full of danger and promise. And these
were the men. I sat up suddenly. A wave of
movement passed through the crowd from end to
end, passed along the heads, swayed the bodies,
ran along the jetty like a ripple on the water, like
a breath of wind on a field—and all was still

again. I see it now—the wide sweep of the bay,
the glittering sands, the wealth of green infinite
and varied, the sea blue like the sea of a dream,
the crowd of attentive faces, the blaze of vivid
colour—the water reflecting it all, the curve of
the shore, the jetty, the high-sterned outlandish
craft floating still, and the three boats with the
tired men from the West sleeping, unconscious
of the land and the people and of the violence of
sunshine. They slept thrown across the thwarts,
curled on bottom-boards, in the careless attitudes
of death. The head of the old skipper, leaning
back in the stern of the long-boat, had fallen on
his breast, and he looked as though he would
never wake. Farther out old Mahon's face was
upturned to the sky, with the long white beard
spread out on his breast, as though he had been
shot where he sat at the tiller; and a man, all in
a heap in the bows of the boat, slept with both
arms embracing the stem-head and with his cheek
laid on the gunwale. The East looked at them
without a sound.

" I have known its fascination since; I have
seen the mysterious shores, the still water, the
lands of brown nations, where a stealthy Nemesis
lies in wait, pursues, overtakes so many of the
conquering race, who are proud of their wisdom,
of their knowledge, of their strength. But for me

all the East is contained in that vision of my
youth. It is all in that moment when I opened
my young eyes on it. I came upon it from a tussle
with the sea—and I was young—and I saw it
looking at me. And this is all that is left of it!
Only a moment; a moment of strength, of
romance, of glamour—of youth! . . . A flick of
sunshine upon a strange shore, the time to remember, the time for a sigh, and—good-bye!—
Night—Good-bye . . .! "

He drank.

" Ah! The good old time—the good old time.
Youth and the sea. Glamour and the sea! The
good, strong sea, the salt, bitter sea, that could
whisper to you and roar at you and knock your
breath out of you."

He drank again.

" By all that's wonderful it is the sea, I believe,
the sea itself—or is it youth alone? Who can
tell? But you here—you all had something out
of life: money, love—whatever one gets on shore
—and, tell me, wasn't that the best time, that
time when we were young at sea; young and
had nothing, on the sea that gives nothing,
except hard knocks—and sometimes a chance
to feel your strength—that only—what you all
regret? "

And we all nodded at him: the man of finance,

the man of accounts, the man of law, we all
nodded at him over the polished table that like a
still sheet of brown water reflected our faces,
lined, wrinkled; our faces marked by toil, by
deceptions, by success, by love; our weary eyes
looking still, looking always, looking anxiously
for something out of life, that while it is expected
is already gone — has passed unseen, in a sigh,
in a flash — together with the youth, with the
strength, with the romance of illusions.

GASPAR RUIZ

GASPAR RUIZ

I

A REVOLUTIONARY war raises many strange characters out of the obscurity which is the common lot of humble lives in an undisturbed state of society.

Certain individualities grow into fame through their vices and their virtues, or simply by their actions, which may have a temporary importance; and then they become forgotten. The names of a few leaders alone survive the end of armed strife and are further preserved in history; so that, vanishing from men's active memories, they still exist in books.

The name of General Santierra attained that cold, paper-and-ink immortality. He was a South American of good family, and the books published in his lifetime numbered him amongst the liberators of that continent from the oppressive rule of Spain.

That long contest, waged for independence on one side and for dominion on the other, developed, in the course of years and the vicissitudes of changing fortune, the fierceness and inhumanity

of a struggle for life. All feelings of pity and
compassion disappeared in the growth of political hatred. And, as is usual in war, the mass
of the people, who had the least to gain by the
issue, suffered most in their obscure persons and
their humble fortunes.

General Santierra began his service as lieutenant in the patriot army raised and commanded
by the famous San Martin, afterwards conqueror
of Lima and liberator of Peru. A great battle
had just been fought on the banks of the river
Bio-Bio. Amongst the prisoners made upon the
routed Royalist troops there was a soldier called
Gaspar Ruiz. His powerful build and his big
head rendered him remarkable amongst his fellow-
captives. The personality of the man was un-
mistakable. Some months before, he had been
missed from the ranks of Republican troops after
one of the many skirmishes which preceded the
great battle. And now, having been captured
arms in hand amongst Royalists, he could expect no other fate but to be shot as a deserter.

Gaspar Ruiz, however, was not a deserter; his
mind was hardly active enough to take a discriminating view of the advantages or perils of
treachery. Why should he change sides? He
had really been made a prisoner, had suffered
ill-usage and many privations. Neither side

showed tenderness to its adversaries. There
came a day when he was ordered, together with
some other captured rebels, to march in the front
rank of the Royal troops. A musket had been
thrust into his hands. He had taken it. He had
marched. He did not want to be killed with
circumstances of peculiar atrocity for refusing
to march. He did not understand heroism, but
it was his intention to throw his musket away
at the first opportunity. Meantime he had gone
on loading and firing, from fear of having his
brains blown out, at the first sign of unwilling-
ness, by some non-commissioned officer of the
King of Spain. He tried to set forth these ele-
mentary considerations before the sergeant of the
guard set over him and some twenty other such
deserters, who had been condemned summarily
to be shot.

It was in the quadrangle of the fort at the
back of the batteries which command the road-
stead of Valparaiso. The officer who had iden-
tified him had gone on without listening to his
protestations. His doom was sealed; his hands
were tied very tightly together behind his back;
his body was sore all over from the many blows
with sticks and butts of muskets which had
hurried him along on the painful road from the
place of his capture to the gate of the fort. This

was the only kind of systematic attention the
prisoners had received from their escort during
a four days' journey across a scantily watered
tract of country. At the crossings of rare streams
they were permitted to quench their thirst by
lapping hurriedly like dogs. In the evening a
few scraps of meat were thrown amongst them
as they dropped down dead-beat upon the stony
ground of the halting-place.

As he stood in the courtyard of the castle in
the early morning, after having been driven hard
all night, Gaspar Ruiz's throat was parched, and
his tongue felt very large and dry in his mouth.

And Gaspar Ruiz, besides being very thirsty,
was stirred by a feeling of sluggish anger, which
he could not very well express, as though the
vigour of his spirit were by no means equal to
the strength of his body.

The other prisoners in the batch of the condemned hung their heads, looking obstinately on
the ground. But Gaspar Ruiz kept on repeating:
" What should I desert for to the Royalists?
Why should I desert? Tell me, Estaban!"

He addressed himself to the sergeant, who
happened to belong to the same part of the
country as himself. But the sergeant, after
shrugging his meagre shoulders once, paid no
further attention to the deep murmuring voice

at his back. It was indeed strange that Gaspar
Ruiz should desert. His people were in too
humble a station to feel much the disadvantages
of any form of government. There was no reason
why Gaspar Ruiz should wish to uphold in his
own person the rule of the King of Spain. Neither
had he been anxious to exert himself for its sub-
version. He had joined the side of Independence
in an extremely reasonable and natural manner.
A band of patriots appeared one morning early,
surrounding his father's ranche, spearing the
watch-dogs and hamstringing a fat cow all in
the twinkling of an eye, to the cries of " *Viva la
Libertad !* " Their officer discoursed of Liberty
with enthusiasm and eloquence after a long and
refreshing sleep. When they left in the evening,
taking with them some of Ruiz, the father's,
best horses to replace their own lamed animals,
Gaspar Ruiz went away with them, having been
invited pressingly to do so by the eloquent officer.

Shortly afterwards a detachment of Royalist
troops, coming to pacify the district, burnt the
ranche, carried off the remaining horses and
cattle, and having thus deprived the old people
of all their worldly possessions, left them sitting
under a bush in the enjoyment of the inestimable
boon of life.

*c

II

GASPAR RUIZ, condemned to death as a deserter, was not thinking either of his native place or of his parents, to whom he had been a good son on account of the mildness of his character and the great strength of his limbs. The practical advantage of this last was made still more valuable to his father by his obedient disposition. Gaspar Ruiz had an acquiescent soul.

But it was stirred now to a sort of dim revolt by his dislike to die the death of a traitor. He was not a traitor. He said again to the sergeant: "You know I did not desert, Estaban. You know I remained behind amongst the trees with three others to keep the enemy back while the detachment was running away!"

Lieutenant Santierra, little more than a boy at the time, and unused as yet to the sanguinary imbecilities of a state of war, had lingered near by, as if fascinated by the sight of these men who were to be shot presently—"for an example"—as the *Commandante* had said.

The sergeant, without deigning to look at the prisoner, addressed himself to the young officer with a superior smile.

" Ten men would not have been enough to
make him a prisoner, *mi teniente*. Moreover, the
other three rejoined the detachment after dark.
Why should he, unwounded and the strongest of
them all, have failed to do so? "

" My strength is as nothing against a mounted
man with a lasso," Gaspar Ruiz protested eagerly.
" He dragged me behind his horse for half a
mile."

At this excellent reason the sergeant only
laughed contemptuously.   The young officer
hurried away after the *Commandante*.

Presently the adjutant of the castle came by.
He was a truculent, raw-boned man in a ragged
uniform.   His spluttering voice issued out of a
flat, yellow face. The sergeant learned from him
that the condemned men would not be shot till
sunset. He begged then to know what he was
to do with them meantime.

The adjutant looked savagely round the courtyard, and, pointing to the door of a small
dungeon-like guard-room, receiving light and
air through one heavily-barred window, said:
" Drive the scoundrels in there."

The sergeant, tightening his grip upon the
stick he carried in virtue of his rank, executed
this order with alacrity and zeal. He hit Gaspar
Ruiz, whose movements were slow, over his head

and shoulders. Gaspar Ruiz stood still for a moment under the shower of blows, biting his lip thoughtfully as if absorbed by a perplexing mental process—then followed the others without haste. The door was locked, and the adjutant carried off the key.

By noon the heat of that low vaulted place crammed to suffocation had become unbearable. The prisoners crowded towards the window, begging their guards for a drop of water; but the soldiers remained lying in indolent attitudes wherever there was a little shade under a wall, while the sentry sat with his back against the door smoking a cigarette, and raising his eyebrows philosophically from time to time. Gaspar Ruiz had pushed his way to the window with irresistible force. His capacious chest needed more air than the others; his big face, resting with its chin on the ledge, pressed close to the bars, seemed to support the other faces crowding up for breath. From moaned entreaties they had passed to desperate cries, and the tumultuous howling of those thirsty men obliged a young officer who was just then crossing the courtyard to shout in order to make himself heard.

"Why don't you give some water to these prisoners!"

The sergeant, with an air of surprised innocence, excused himself by the remark that all those men were condemned to die in a very few hours.

Lieutenant Santierra stamped his foot. "They are condemned to death, not to torture," he shouted. "Give them some water at once."

Impressed by this appearance of anger, the soldiers bestirred themselves, and the sentry, snatching up his musket, stood to attention.

But when a couple of buckets were found and filled from the well, it was discovered that they could not be passed through the bars, which were set too close. At the prospect of quenching their thirst, the shrieks of those trampled down in the struggle to get near the opening became very heartrending. But when the soldiers who had lifted the buckets towards the window put them to the ground again helplessly, the yell of disappointment was still more terrible.

The soldiers of the army of Independence were not equipped with canteens. A small tin cup was found, but its approach to the opening caused such a commotion, such yells of rage and pain in the vague mass of limbs behind the straining faces at the window, that Lieutenant Santierra cried out hurriedly, "No, no — you must open the door, sergeant."

The sergeant, shrugging his shoulders, ex-

plained that he had no right to open the door
even if he had had the key. But he had not the
key. The adjutant of the garrison kept the key.
Those men were giving much unnecessary trouble,
since they had to die at sunset in any case. Why
they had not been shot at once early in the morning he could not understand.

Lieutenant Santierra kept his back studiously
to the window. It was at his earnest solicita-
tions that the *Commandante* had delayed the
execution. This favour had been granted to him
in consideration of his distinguished family and
of his father's high position amongst the chiefs
of the Republican party. Lieutenant Santierra
believed that the General commanding would
visit the fort some time in the afternoon, and
he ingenuously hoped that his naïve intercession
would induce that severe man to pardon some,
at least, of those criminals. In the revulsion of
his feeling his interference stood revealed now
as guilty and futile meddling. It appeared to
him obvious that the general would never even
consent to listen to his petition. He could never
save those men, and he had only made himself
responsible for the sufferings added to the cruelty
of their fate.

" Then go at once and get the key from the
adjutant," said Lieutenant Santierra.

The sergeant shook his head with a sort of bashful smile, while his eyes glanced sideways at Gaspar Ruiz's face, motionless and silent, staring through the bars at the bottom of a heap of other haggard, distorted, yelling faces.

His worship the adjutant de Plaza, the sergeant murmured, was having his siesta; and supposing that he, the sergeant, would be allowed access to him, the only result he expected would be to have his soul flogged out of his body for presuming to disturb his worship's repose. He made a deprecatory movement with his hands, and stood stock-still, looking down modestly upon his brown toes.

Lieutenant Santierra glared with indignation, but hesitated. His handsome oval face, as smooth as a girl's, flushed with the shame of his perplexity. Its nature humiliated his spirit. His hairless upper lip trembled; he seemed on the point of either bursting into a fit of rage or into tears of dismay.

Fifty years later, General Santierra, the venerable relic of revolutionary times, was well able to remember the feelings of the young lieutenant. Since he had given up riding altogether, and found it difficult to walk beyond the limits of his garden, the general's greatest delight was to entertain in his house the officers of the foreign

men-of-war visiting the harbour. For Englishmen he had a preference, as for old companions
in arms. English naval men of all ranks accepted
his hospitality with curiosity, because he had
known Lord Cochrane and had taken part, on
board the patriot squadron commanded by that
marvellous seaman, in the cutting-out and block-
ading operations before Callao—an episode of
unalloyed glory in the wars of Independence and
of endless honour in the fighting tradition of
Englishmen. He was a fair linguist, this ancient
survivor of the Liberating armies. A trick of
smoothing his long white beard whenever he was
short of a word in French or English imparted
an air of leisurely dignity to the tone of his
reminiscences.

III

"Yes, my friends," he used to say to his guests,
"what would you have? A youth of seventeen
summers, without worldly experience, and owing
my rank only to the glorious patriotism of my
father, may God rest his soul, I suffered immense
humiliation, not so much from the disobedience
of that subordinate, who, after all, was responsible for those prisoners; but I suffered because,

like the boy I was, I myself dreaded going to the adjutant for the key. I had felt, before, his rough and cutting tongue. Being quite a common fellow, with no merit except his savage valour, he made me feel his contempt and dislike from the first day I joined my battalion in garrison at the fort. It was only a fortnight before! I would have confronted him sword in hand, but I shrank from the mocking brutality of his sneers.

" I don't remember having been so miserable in my life before or since. The torment of my sensibility was so great that I wished the sergeant to fall dead at my feet, and the stupid soldiers who stared at me to turn into corpses; and even those wretches for whom my entreaties had procured a reprieve I wished dead also, because I could not face them without shame. A mephitic heat like a whiff of air from hell came out of that dark place in which they were confined. Those at the window who heard what was going on jeered at me in very desperation; one of these fellows, gone mad no doubt, kept on urging me volubly to order the soldiers to fire through the window. His insane loquacity made my heart turn faint. And my feet were like lead. There was no higher officer to whom I could appeal. I had not even the firmness of spirit to simply go away.

"Benumbed by my remorse, I stood with my back to the window. You must not suppose that all this lasted a long time. How long could it have been? A minute? If you measured by mental suffering it was like a hundred years; a longer time than all my life has been since. No, certainly, it was not so much as a minute. The hoarse screaming of those miserable wretches died out in their dry throats, and then suddenly a voice spoke, a deep voice muttering calmly. It called upon me to turn round.

"That voice, señores, proceeded from the head of Gaspar Ruiz. Of his body I could see nothing. Some of his fellow-captives had clambered upon his back. He was holding them up. His eyes blinked without looking at me. That and the moving of his lips was all he seemed able to manage in his overloaded state. And when I turned round, this head, that seemed more than human size resting on its chin under a multitude of other heads, asked me whether I really desired to quench the thirst of the captives.

"I said, 'Yes, yes!' eagerly, and came up quite close to the window. I was like a child, and did not know what would happen. I was anxious to be comforted in my helplessness and remorse.

"'Have you the authority, *señor teniente*, to

release my wrists from their bonds?' Gaspar
Ruiz's head asked me.

"His features expressed no anxiety, no hope;
his heavy eyelids blinked upon his eyes that
looked past me straight into the courtyard.

"As if in an ugly dream, I spoke, stammering:
'What do you mean? And how can I reach the
bonds on your wrists?'

"'I will try what I can do,' he said; and
then that large staring head moved at last, and
all the wild faces piled up in that window disappeared, tumbling down. He had shaken his
load off with one movement, so strong he was.

"And he had not only shaken it off, but he
got free of the crush and vanished from my
sight. For a moment there was no one at all to
be seen at the window. He had swung about,
butting and shouldering, clearing a space for
himself in the only way he could do it with his
hands tied behind his back.

"Finally, backing to the opening, he pushed
out to me between the bars his wrists, lashed
with many turns of rope. His hands, very
swollen, with knotted veins, looked enormous
and unwieldy. I saw his bent back. It was
very broad. His voice was like the muttering
of a bull.

"'Cut, *señor teniente!* Cut!'

" I drew my sword, my new unblunted sword that had seen no service as yet, and severed the many turns of the hide rope. I did this without knowing the why and the wherefore of my action, but as it were compelled by my faith in that man. The sergeant made as if to cry out, but astonishment deprived him of his voice, and he remained standing with his mouth open as if overtaken by sudden imbecility.

" I sheathed my sword and faced the soldiers. An air of awestruck expectation had replaced their usual listless apathy. I heard the voice of Gaspar Ruiz shouting inside, but the words I could not make out plainly. I suppose that to see him with his arms free augmented the influence of his strength: I mean by this, the spiritual influence that with ignorant people attaches to an exceptional degree of bodily vigour. In fact, he was no more to be feared than before, on account of the numbness of his arms and hands, which lasted for some time.

" The sergeant had recovered his power of speech. ' By all the saints ! ' he cried, ' we shall have to get a cavalry man with a lasso to secure him again, if he is to be led to the place of execution. Nothing less than a good *enlazador* on a good horse can subdue him. Your worship was pleased to perform a very mad thing.'

"I had nothing to say. I was surprised myself, and I felt a childish curiosity to see what would happen. But the sergeant was thinking of the difficulty of controlling Gaspar Ruiz when the time for making an example would come.

"'Or perhaps,' the sergeant pursued vexedly, 'we shall be obliged to shoot him down as he dashes out when the door is opened.' He was going to give further vent to his anxieties as to the proper carrying out of the sentence; but he interrupted himself with a sudden exclamation, snatched a musket from a soldier, and stood watchful with his eyes fixed on the window

IV

"GASPAR RUIZ had clambered up on the sill, and sat down there with his feet against the thickness of the wall and his knees slightly bent. The window was not quite broad enough for the length of his legs. It appeared to my crestfallen perception that he meant to keep the window all to himself. He seemed to be taking up a comfortable position. Nobody inside dared to approach him now he could strike with his hands.

"'Por Dios!' I heard the sergeant muttering

at my elbow, ' I shall shoot him through the head now, and get rid of that trouble. He is a condemned man.'

"At that I looked at him angrily. ' The general has not confirmed the sentence,' I said— though I knew well in my heart that these were but vain words. The sentence required no confirmation. ' You have no right to shoot him unless he tries to escape,' I added firmly.

"' But *sangre de Dios!*' the sergeant yelled out, bringing his musket up to the shoulder, ' he is escaping now. Look!'

"But I, as if that Gaspar Ruiz had cast a spell upon me, struck the musket upward, and the bullet flew over the roofs somewhere. The sergeant dashed his arm to the ground and stared. He might have commanded the soldiers to fire, but he did not. And if he had he would not have been obeyed, I think, just then.

"With his feet against the thickness of the wall, and his hairy hands grasping the iron bar, Gaspar sat still. It was an attitude. Nothing happened for a time. And suddenly it dawned upon us that he was straightening his bowed back and contracting his arms. His lips were twisted into a snarl. Next thing we perceived was that the bar of forged iron was being bent slowly by the mightiness of his pull. The sun was beating full upon his cramped, unquivering figure. A shower of sweat-drops burst out of his forehead. Watching the bar grow crooked, I saw a little blood ooze from under his finger-nails. Then he let go. For a moment he remained all huddled up, with a hanging head, looking drowsily into the upturned palms of his mighty hands. Indeed he seemed to have dozed off. Suddenly he flung himself backwards on the sill, and setting the soles of his bare feet against the other middle bar, he bent that one too, but in the opposite direction from the first.

" Such was his strength, which in this case relieved my painful feelings. And the man seemed to have done nothing. Except for the change of position in order to use his feet, which made us all start by its swiftness, my recollection is that of immobility. But he had bent the bars wide apart. And now he could get out if he liked; but he dropped his legs inwards, and looking over his shoulder beckoned to the soldiers. ' Hand up the water,' he said. ' I will give them all a drink.'

" He was obeyed. For a moment I expected man and bucket to disappear, overwhelmed by the rush of eagerness; I thought they would pull him down with their teeth. There was a rush, but holding the bucket on his lap he

repulsed the assault of those wretches by the
mere swinging of his feet. They flew backwards
at every kick, yelling with pain; and the soldiers
laughed, gazing at the window.

"They all laughed, holding their sides, except
the sergeant, who was gloomy and morose. He
was afraid the prisoners would rise and break
out—which would have been a bad example.
But there was no fear of that, and I stood myself before the window with my drawn sword.
When sufficiently tamed by the strength of
Gaspar Ruiz, they came up one by one, stretching their necks and presenting their lips to the
edge of the bucket which the strong man tilted
towards them from his knees with an extraordinary air of charity, gentleness and compassion. That benevolent appearance was of course
the effect of his care in not spilling the water
and of his attitude as he sat on the sill; for,
if a man lingered with his lips glued to the rim
of the bucket after Gaspar Ruiz had said ' You
have had enough,' there would be no tenderness
or mercy in the shove of the foot which would
send him groaning and doubled up far into the
interior of the prison, where he would knock
down two or three others before he fell himself.
They came up to him again and again; it looked
as if they meant to drink the well dry before

going to their death; but the soldiers were so
amused by Gaspar Ruiz's systematic proceedings
that they carried the water up to the window
cheerfully.

"When the adjutant came out after his siesta
there was some trouble over this affair, I can
assure you. And the worst of it, that the general
whom we expected never came to the castle
that day."

The guests of General Santierra unanimously
expressed their regret that the man of such
strength and patience had not been saved.

"He was not saved by my interference," said
the General. "The prisoners were led to execution half an hour before sunset. Gaspar Ruiz,
contrary to the sergeant's apprehensions, gave
no trouble. There was no necessity to get a
cavalry man with a lasso in order to subdue
him, as if he were a wild bull of the *campo*. I
believe he marched out with his arms free
amongst the others who were bound. I did not
see. I was not there. I had been put under
arrest for interfering with the prisoner's guard.
About dusk, sitting dismally in my quarters, I
heard three volleys fired, and thought that I
should never hear of Gaspar Ruiz again. He fell
with the others. But we were to hear of him
nevertheless, though the sergeant boasted that,

as he lay on his face expiring or dead in the
heap of the slain, he had slashed his neck with
a sword. He had done this, he said, to make
sure of ridding the world of a dangerous traitor.

"I confess to you, señores, that I thought of
that strong man with a sort of gratitude, and
with some admiration. He had used his strength
honourably. There dwelt, then, in his soul no
fierceness corresponding to the vigour of his
body."

V

GASPAR RUIZ, who could with ease bend apart
the heavy iron bars of the prison, was led out
with others to summary execution. "Every
bullet has its billet," runs the proverb. All the
merit of proverbs consists in the concise and
picturesque expression. In the surprise of our
minds is found their persuasiveness. In other
words, we are struck and convinced by the shock.

What surprises us is the form, not the sub-
stance. Proverbs are art—cheap art. As a general
rule they are not true; unless indeed they happen to be mere platitudes, as for instance the
proverb, "Half a loaf is better than no bread,"

or " A miss is as good as a mile." Some proverbs are simply imbecile, others are immoral. That one evolved out of the naïve heart of the great Russian people, " Man discharges the piece, but God carries the bullet," is piously atrocious, and at bitter variance with the accepted conception of a compassionate God. It would indeed be an inconsistent occupation for the Guardian of the poor, the innocent and the helpless, to carry the bullet, for instance, into the heart of a father.

Gaspar Ruiz was childless, he had no wife, he had never been in love. He had hardly ever spoken to a woman, beyond his mother and the ancient negress of the household, whose wrinkled skin was the colour of cinders, and whose lean body was bent double from age. If some bullets from those muskets fired off at fifteen paces were specifically destined for the heart of Gaspar Ruiz, they all missed their billet. One, however, carried away a small piece of his ear, and another a fragment of flesh from his shoulder.

A red and unclouded sun setting into a purple ocean looked with a fiery stare upon the enormous wall of the Cordilleras, worthy witnesses of his glorious extinction. But it is inconceivable that it should have seen the ant-like men busy with their absurd and insignificant trials of killing and dying for reasons that, apart from being generally childish, were also imperfectly understood. It did light up, however, the backs of the firing party and the faces of the condemned men. Some of them had fallen on their knees, others remained standing, a few averted their heads from the levelled barrels of muskets. Gaspar Ruiz, upright, the burliest of them all, hung his big shock head. The low sun dazzled him a little, and he counted himself a dead man already.

He fell at the first discharge. He fell because he thought he was a dead man. He struck the ground heavily. The jar of the fall surprised him. " I am not dead apparently," he thought to himself, when he heard the execution platoon reloading its arms at the word of command. It was then that the hope of escape dawned upon him for the first time. He remained lying stretched out with rigid limbs under the weight of two bodies collapsed crosswise upon his back.

By the time the soldiers had fired a third volley into the slightly stirring heaps of the slain, the sun had gone out of sight, and almost immediately with the darkening of the ocean dusk fell upon the coasts of the young Republic. Above the gloom of the lowlands the snowy peaks of the Cordillera remained luminous and crimson for a long time. The soldiers before marching back to the fort sat down to smoke.

The sergeant with a naked sword in his hand strolled away by himself along the heap of the dead. He was a humane man, and watched for any stir or twitch of limb in the merciful idea of plunging the point of his blade into any body giving the slightest sign of life. But none of the bodies afforded him an opportunity for the display of this charitable intention. Not a muscle twitched amongst them, not even the powerful muscles of Gaspar Ruiz, who, deluged with the blood of his neighbours and shamming death, strove to appear more lifeless than the others.

He was lying face down. The sergeant recognised him by his stature, and being himself a very small man, looked with envy and contempt at the prostration of so much strength. He had always disliked that particular soldier. Moved by an obscure animosity, he inflicted a long gash across the neck of Gaspar Ruiz, with some vague notion of making sure of that strong man's death, as if a powerful physique were more able to resist the bullets. For the sergeant had no doubt that Gaspar Ruiz had been shot through in many places. Then he passed on, and shortly afterwards marched off with his men, leaving the bodies to the care of crows and vultures.

Gaspar Ruiz had restrained a cry, though it had seemed to him that his head was cut off at a blow; and when darkness came, shaking off the dead, whose weight had oppressed him, he crawled away over the plain on his hands and knees. After drinking deeply, like a wounded beast, at a shallow stream, he assumed an upright posture, and staggered on light-headed and aimless, as if lost amongst the stars of the clear night. A small house seemed to rise out of the ground before him. He stumbled into the porch and struck at the door with his fist. There was not a gleam of light. Gaspar Ruiz might have thought that the inhabitants had fled from it, as from many others in the neighbourhood, had it not been for the shouts of abuse that answered his thumping. In his feverish and enfeebled state the angry screaming seemed to him part of a hallucination belonging to the weird dreamlike feeling of his unexpected condemnation to death, of the thirst suffered, of the volleys fired at him within fifteen paces, of his head being cut off at a blow. " Open the door! " he cried. " Open in the name of God! "

An infuriated voice from within jeered at him: " Come in, come in. This house belongs to you. All this land belongs to you. Come and take it."

" For the love of God," Gaspar Ruiz murmured.

" Does not all the land belong to you patriots?" the voice on the other side of the door screamed on. " Are you not a patriot? "

Gaspar Ruiz did not know. " I am a wounded man," he said apathetically.

All became still inside. Gaspar Ruiz lost the hope of being admitted, and lay down under the porch just outside the door. He was utterly careless of what was going to happen to him. All his consciousness seemed to be concentrated in his neck, where he felt a severe pain. His indifference as to his fate was genuine.

The day was breaking when he awoke from a feverish doze; the door at which he had knocked in the dark stood wide open now, and a girl, steadying herself with her outspread arms, leaned over the threshold. Lying on his back, he stared up at her. Her face was pale and her eyes were very dark; her hair hung down black as ebony against her white cheeks; her lips were full and red. Beyond her he saw another head with long grey hair, and a thin old face with a pair of anxiously clasped hands under the chin.

VI

" I KNEW those people by sight," General Santierra would tell his guests at the dining-table.
" I mean the people with whom Gaspar Ruiz
found shelter. The father was an old Spaniard,
a man of property, ruined by the revolution.
His estates, his house in town, his money, everything he had in the world had been confiscated
by proclamation, for he was a bitter foe of our
independence. From a position of great dignity
and influence on the Viceroy's Council he became
of less importance than his own negro slaves
made free by our glorious revolution. He had
not even the means to flee the country, as other
Spaniards had managed to do. It may be that,
wandering ruined and houseless, and burdened
with nothing but his life, which was left to him
by the clemency of the Provisional Government,
he had simply walked under that broken roof of
old tiles. It was a lonely spot. There did not
seem to be even a dog belonging to the place.
But though the roof had holes, as if a cannon-
ball or two had dropped through it, the wooden
shutters were thick and tight-closed all the
time.

" My way took me frequently along the path in front of that miserable rancho. I rode from the fort to the town almost every evening, to sigh at the window of a lady I was in love with, then. When one is young, you understand. . . . She was a good patriot, you may be sure. *Caballeros*, credit me or not, political feeling ran so high in those days that I do not believe I could have been fascinated by the charms of a woman of Royalist opinions. . . ."

Murmurs of amused incredulity all round the table interrupted the General; and while they lasted he stroked his white beard gravely.

" Señores," he protested, " a Royalist was a monster to our overwrought feelings. I am telling you this in order not to be suspected of the slightest tenderness towards that old Royalist's daughter. Moreover, as you know, my affections were engaged elsewhere. But I could not help noticing her on rare occasions when with the front door open she stood in the porch.

" You must know that this old Royalist was as crazy as a man can be. His political misfortunes, his total downfall and ruin, had disordered his mind. To show his contempt for what we patriots could do, he affected to laugh at his imprisonment, at the confiscation of his lands, the burning of his houses, and the misery

D

to which he and his womenfolk were reduced.
This habit of laughing had grown upon him, so
that he would begin to laugh and shout directly
he caught sight of any stranger. That was the
form of his madness.

" I, of course, disregarded the noise of that
madman with that feeling of superiority the success of our cause inspired in us Americans. I
suppose I really despised him because he was an
old Castilian, a Spaniard born, and a Royalist.
Those were certainly no reasons to scorn a man;
but for centuries Spaniards born had shown
their contempt of us Americans, men as well
descended as themselves, simply because we were
what they called colonists. We had been kept
in abasement and made to feel our inferiority in
social intercourse. And now it was our turn. It
was safe for us patriots to display the same
sentiments ; and I being a young patriot, son
of a patriot, despised that old Spaniard, and
despising him I naturally disregarded his abuse,
though it was annoying to my feelings. Others
perhaps would not have been so forbearing.

" He would begin with a great yell—' I see a
patriot. Another of them!' long before I came
abreast of the house. The tone of his senseless
revilings, mingled with bursts of laughter, was
sometimes piercingly shrill and sometimes grave.

It was all very mad; but I felt it incumbent
upon my dignity to check my horse to a walk
without even glancing towards the house, as if
that man's abusive clamour in the porch were
less than the barking of a cur. I rode by, pre-
serving an expression of haughty indifference on
my face.

" It was no doubt very dignified; but I should
have done better if I had kept my eyes open.
A military man in war time should never consider himself off duty; and especially so if the
war is a revolutionary war, when the enemy is
not at the door, but within your very house. At
such times the heat of passionate convictions,
passing into hatred, removes the restraints of
honour and humanity from many men and of
delicacy and fear from some women. These last,
when once they throw off the timidity and reserve of their sex, become by the vivacity of
their intelligence and the violence of their merci-
less resentment more dangerous than so many
armed giants."

The General's voice rose, but his big hand
stroked his white beard twice with an effect of
venerable calmness. " *Si, señores!* Women are
ready to rise to the heights of devotion un-
attainable by us men, or to sink into the
depths of abasement which amazes our masculine

prejudices. I am speaking now of exceptional women, you understand. . . ."

Here one of the guests observed that he had never met a woman yet who was not capable of turning out quite exceptional under circumstances that would engage her feelings strongly. "That sort of superiority in recklessness they have over us," he concluded, "makes of them the more interesting half of mankind."

The General, who bore the interruption with gravity, nodded courteous assent. "*Si. Si.* Under circumstances. . . . Precisely. They can do an infinite deal of mischief sometimes in quite unexpected ways. For who could have imagined that a young girl, daughter of a ruined Royalist whose life itself was held only by the contempt of his enemies, would have had the power to bring death and devastation upon two flourishing provinces and cause serious anxiety to the leaders of the revolution in the very hour of its success!" He paused to let the wonder of it penetrate our minds.

"Death and devastation," somebody murmured in surprise: "how shocking!"

The old General gave a glance in the direction of the murmur and went on. "Yes. That is, war—calamity. But the means by which she obtained the power to work this havoc on our southern frontier seem to me, who have seen her and spoken to her, still more shocking. That particular thing left on my mind a dreadful amazement which the further experience of life, of more than fifty years, has done nothing to diminish." He looked round as if to make sure of our attention, and, in a changed voice: " I am, as you know, a republican, son of a Liberator," he declared. " My incomparable mother, God rest her soul, was a Frenchwoman, the daughter of an ardent republican. As a boy I fought for liberty; I've always believed in the equality of men; and as to their brotherhood, that, to my mind, is even more certain. Look at the fierce animosity they display in their differences. And what in the world do you know that is more bitterly fierce than brothers' quarrels? "

All absence of cynicism checked an inclination to smile at this view of human brotherhood. On the contrary, there was in the tone the melancholy natural to a man profoundly humane at heart who from duty, from conviction and from necessity, had played his part in scenes of ruthless violence.

The General had seen much of fratricidal strife. " Certainly. There is no doubt of their brotherhood," he insisted. " All men are brothers, and

as such know almost too much of each other.
But "—and here in the old patriarchal head,
white as silver, the black eyes humorously
twinkled—" if we are all brothers, all the women
are not our sisters."

One of the younger guests was heard murmuring his satisfaction at the fact. But the
General continued, with deliberate earnestness:
" They are so different! The tale of a king who
took a beggar-maid for a partner of his throne
may be pretty enough as we men look upon
ourselves and upon love. But that a young girl,
famous for her haughty beauty and, only a short
time before, the admired of all at the balls in
the Viceroy's palace, should take by the hand a
guasso, a common peasant, is intolerable to our
sentiment of women and their love. It is madness. Nevertheless it happened. But it must
be said that in her case it was the madness of
hate—not of love."

After presenting this excuse in a spirit of
chivalrous justice, the General remained silent
for a time. " I rode past the house every day
almost," he began again, " and this was what
was going on within. But how it was going on
no mind of man can conceive. Her desperation
must have been extreme, and Gaspar Ruiz was
a docile fellow. He had been an obedient soldier.

His strength was like an enormous stone lying on the ground, ready to be hurled this way or that by the hand that picks it up.

" It is clear that he would tell his story to the people who gave him the shelter he needed. And he needed assistance badly. His wound was not dangerous, but his life was forfeited. The old Royalist being wrapped up in his laughing madness, the two women arranged a hiding-place for the wounded man in one of the huts amongst the fruit trees at the back of the house. That hovel, an abundance of clear water while the fever was on him, and some words of pity were all they could give. I suppose he had a share of what food there was. And it would be but little; a handful of roasted corn, perhaps a dish of beans, or a piece of bread with a few figs. To such misery were those proud and once wealthy people reduced."

VII

GENERAL SANTIERRA was right in his surmise. Such was the exact nature of the assistance which Gaspar Ruiz, peasant son of peasants, received from the Royalist family whose daughter had opened the door of their miserable refuge to his extreme distress. Her sombre resolution ruled the madness of her father and the trembling bewilderment of her mother.

She had asked the strange man on the doorstep, " Who wounded you? "

" The soldiers, señora," Gaspar Ruiz had answered, in a faint voice.

" Patriots? "

" *Si.*"

" What for? "

" Deserter," he gasped, leaning against the wall under the scrutiny of her black eyes. " I was left for dead over there."

She led him through the house out to a small hut of clay and reeds, lost in the long grass of the overgrown orchard. He sank on a heap of maize straw in a corner, and sighed profoundly.

" No one will look for you here," she said, looking down at him. " Nobody comes near us. We too have been left for dead—here."

He stirred uneasily on his heap of dirty straw, and the pain in his neck made him groan deliriously.

" I shall show Estaban some day that I am alive yet," he mumbled.

He accepted her assistance in silence, and the many days of pain went by. Her appearances in the hut brought him relief and became connected with the feverish dreams of angels which visited his couch; for Gaspar Ruiz was instructed in the mysteries of his religion, and had even been taught to read and write a little by the priest of his village. He waited for her with impatience, and saw her pass out of the dark hut and disappear in the brilliant sunshine with poignant regret. He discovered that, while he lay there feeling so very weak, he could, by closing his eyes, evoke her face with considerable distinctness. And this discovered faculty charmed the long solitary hours of his convalescence. Later, when he began to regain his strength, he would creep at dusk from his hut to the house and sit on the step of the garden door.

In one of the rooms the mad father paced to and fro, muttering to himself with short abrupt laughs. In the passage, sitting on a stool, the mother sighed and moaned. The daughter, in rough threadbare clothing, and her white haggard face half hidden by a coarse *manta*, stood leaning against the lintel of the door. Gaspar Ruiz, with his elbows propped on his knees and his head resting in his hands, talked to the two women in an undertone.

The common misery of destitution would have made a bitter mockery of a marked insistence

*D

on social differences. Gaspar Ruiz understood
this in his simplicity. From his captivity amongst
the Royalists he could give them news of people
they knew. He described their appearance; and
when he related the story of the battle in which
he was recaptured the two women lamented the
blow to their cause and the ruin of their secret
hopes.

He had no feeling either way. But he felt
a great devotion for that young girl. In his
desire to appear worthy of her condescension, he
boasted a little of his bodily strength. He had
nothing else to boast of. Because of that quality
his comrades treated him with as great a defer-
ence, he explained, as though he had been a
sergeant, both in camp and in battle.

" I could always get as many as I wanted to
follow me anywhere, señorita. I ought to have
been made an officer, because I can read and
write."

Behind him the silent old lady fetched a
moaning sigh from time to time; the distracted
father muttered to himself, pacing the *sala*; and
Gaspar Ruiz would raise his eyes now and then
to look at the daughter of these people.

He would look at her with curiosity because
she was alive, and also with that feeling of famili-
arity and awe with which he had contemplated

in churches the inanimate and powerful statues
of the saints, whose protection is invoked in
dangers and difficulties. His difficulty was very
great.

He could not remain hiding in an orchard for
ever and ever. He knew also very well that before
he had gone half a day's journey in any direction,
he would be picked up by one of the cavalry
patrols scouring the country, and brought into
one or another of the camps where the patriot
army destined for the liberation of Peru was
collected. There he would in the end be recognised as Gaspar Ruiz—the deserter to the Royalists—and no doubt shot very effectually this
time. There did not seem any place in the world
for the innocent Gaspar Ruiz anywhere. And
at this thought his simple soul surrendered itself
to gloom and resentment as black as night.

They had made him a soldier forcibly. He
did not mind being a soldier. And he had been
a good soldier as he had been a good son, because of his docility and his strength. But now
there was no use for either. They had taken
him from his parents, and he could no longer
be a soldier—not a good soldier at any rate.
Nobody would listen to his explanations. What
injustice it was! What injustice!

And in a mournful murmur he would go over

the story of his capture and recapture for the
twentieth time. Then, raising his eyes to the
silent girl in the doorway, " *Si, señorita*," he
would say with a deep sigh, " injustice has made
this poor breath in my body quite worthless to
me and to anybody else. And I do not care who
robs me of it."

One evening, as he exhaled thus the plaint of
his wounded soul, she condescended to say that,
if she were a man, she would consider no life
worthless which held the possibility of revenge.

She seemed to be speaking to herself. Her
voice was low. He drank in the gentle, as if
dreamy sound, with a consciousness of peculiar
delight, of something warming his breast like a
draught of generous wine.

" True, señorita," he said, raising his face up
to hers slowly: " there is Estaban, who must be
shown that I am not dead after all."

The mutterings of the mad father had ceased
long before; the sighing mother had withdrawn
somewhere into one of the empty rooms. All
was still within as well as without, in the moonlight bright as day on the wild orchard full of
inky shadows. Gaspar Ruiz saw the dark eyes
of Doña Erminia look down at him.

" Ah! The sergeant," she muttered disdain-
fully.

"Why! He has wounded me with his sword," he protested, bewildered by the contempt that seemed to shine livid on her pale face.

She crushed him with her glance. The power of her will to be understood was so strong that it kindled in him the intelligence of unexpressed things.

"What else did you expect me to do?" he cried, as if suddenly driven to despair. "Have I the power to do more? Am I a general with an army at my back?—miserable sinner that I am to be despised by you at last."

VIII

"Señores," related the General to his guests, "though my thoughts were of love then, and therefore enchanting, the sight of that house always affected me disagreeably, especially in the moonlight, when its close shutters and its air of lonely neglect appeared sinister. Still I went on using the bridle-path by the ravine, because it was a short cut. The mad Royalist howled and laughed at me every evening to his complete satisfaction; but after a time, as if wearied with my indifference, he ceased to

appear in the porch. How they persuaded him to
leave off I do not know. However, with Gaspar
Ruiz in the house there would have been no
difficulty in restraining him by force. It was
part of their policy in there to avoid anything which could provoke me. At least, so I
suppose.

"Notwithstanding my infatuation with the
brighest pair of eyes in Chile, I noticed the absence of the old man after a week or so. A few
more days passed. I began to think that perhaps
these Royalists had gone away somewhere else.
But one evening, as I was hastening towards the
city, I saw again somebody in the porch. It was
not the madman; it was the girl. She stood
holding on to one of the wooden columns, tall
and white-faced, her big eyes sunk deep with
privation and sorrow. I looked hard at her, and
she met my stare with a strange, inquisitive
look. Then, as I turned my head after riding
past, she seemed to gather courage for the act,
and absolutely beckoned me back.

"I obeyed, señores, almost without thinking,
so great was my astonishment. It was greater
still when I heard what she had to say. She
began by thanking me for my forbearance of
her father's infirmity, so that I felt ashamed of
myself. I had meant to show disdain, not for-

bearance! Every word must have burnt her
lips, but she never departed from a gentle and
melancholy dignity which filled me with respect
against my will. Señores, we are no match for
women. But I could hardly believe my ears
when she began her tale. Providence, she concluded, seemed to have preserved the life of that
wronged soldier, who now trusted to my honour
as a *caballero* and to my compassion for his
sufferings.

" ' Wronged man,' I observed coldly. ' Well,
I think so too: and you have been harbouring
an enemy of your cause.'

" ' He was a poor Christian crying for help at
our door in the name of God, señor,' she answered
simply.

" I began to admire her. ' Where is he now? '
I asked stiffly.

" But she would not answer that question.
With extreme cunning, and an almost fiendish
delicacy, she managed to remind me of my
failure in saving the lives of the prisoners in the
guard-room, without wounding my pride. She
knew, of course, the whole story. Gaspar Ruiz,
she said, entreated me to procure for him a safe-
conduct from General San Martin himself. He
had an important communication to make to
the Commander-in-Chief.

"*Por Dios, señores*, she made me swallow all that, pretending to be only the mouthpiece of that poor man. Overcome by injustice, he expected to find, she said, as much generosity in me as had been shown to him by the Royalist family which had given him a refuge.

"Ha! It was well and nobly said to a youngster like me. I thought her great. Alas! she was only implacable.

"In the end I rode away very enthusiastic about the business, without demanding even to see Gaspar Ruiz, who I was confident was in the house.

"But on calm reflection I began to see some difficulties which I had not confidence enough in myself to encounter. It was not easy to approach a commander-in-chief with such a story. I feared failure. At last I thought it better to lay the matter before my general-of-division, Robles, a friend of my family, who had appointed me his aide-de-camp lately.

"He took it out of my hands at once without any ceremony.

"'In the house! of course he is in the house,' he said contemptuously. 'You ought to have gone sword in hand inside and demanded his surrender, instead of chatting with a Royalist girl in the porch. Those people should have

been hunted out of that long ago. Who knows
how many spies they have harboured right in
the very midst of our camps? A safe-conduct
from the Commander-in-Chief! The audacity of
the fellow! Ha! ha! Now we shall catch him
to-night, and then we shall find out, without any
safe-conduct, what he has got to say, that is so
very important. Ha! ha! ha!'

"General Robles, peace to his soul, was a
short, thick man, with round, staring eyes,
fierce and jovial. Seeing my distress he
added:

"'Come, come, *chico*. I promise you his life
if he does not resist. And that is not likely.
We are not going to break up a good soldier if
it can be helped. I tell you what! I am curious
to see your strong man. Nothing but a general
will do for the *picaro*—well, he shall have a
general to talk to. Ha! ha! I shall go myself
to the catching, and you are coming with me, of
course.'

"And it was done that same night. Early in
the evening the house and the orchard were
surrounded quietly. Later on the general and
I left a ball we were attending in town and rode
out at an easy gallop. At some little distance
from the house we pulled up. A mounted orderly
held our horses. A low whistle warned the men

watching all along the ravine, and we walked up
to the porch softly. The barricaded house in
the moonlight seemed empty.

"The general knocked at the door. After a
time a woman's voice within asked who was
there. My chief nudged me hard. I gasped.

"'It is I, Lieutenant Santierra,' I stammered
out, as if choked. 'Open the door.'

"It came open slowly. The girl, holding a
thin taper in her hand, seeing another man with
me, began to back away before us slowly, shad-
ing the light with her hand. Her impassive
white face looked ghostly. I followed behind
General Robles. Her eyes were fixed on mine.
I made a gesture of helplessness behind my
chief's back, trying at the same time to give a
reassuring expression to my face. Neither of us
three uttered a sound.

"We found ourselves in a room with bare floor
and walls. There was a rough table and a couple
of stools in it, nothing else whatever. An old
woman with her grey hair hanging loose wrung
her hands when we appeared. A peal of loud
laughter resounded through the empty house,
very amazing and weird. At this the old woman
tried to get past us.

"'Nobody to leave the room,' said General
Robles to me.

"I swung the door to, heard the latch click, and the laughter became faint in our ears.

"Before another word could be spoken in that room I was amazed by hearing the sound of distant thunder.

"I had carried in with me into the house a vivid impression of a beautiful, clear, moonlight night, without a speck of cloud in the sky. I could not believe my ears. Sent early abroad for my education, I was not familiar with the most dreaded natural phenomenon of my native land. I saw, with inexpressible astonishment, a look of terror in my chief's eyes. Suddenly I felt giddy! The general staggered against me heavily; the girl seemed to reel in the middle of the room, the taper fell out of her hand and the light went out; a shrill cry of *Misericordia!* from the old woman pierced my ears. In the pitchy darkness I heard the plaster off the walls falling on the floor. It is a mercy there was no ceiling. Holding on to the latch of the door, I heard the grinding of the roof-tiles cease above my head. The shock was over.

"'Out of the house! The door! Fly, Santierra, fly!' howled the general. You know, señores, in our country the bravest are not ashamed of the fear an earthquake strikes into all the senses of man. One never gets used to it.

Repeated experience only augments the mastery of that nameless terror.

" It was my first earthquake, and I was the calmest of them all. I understood that the crash outside was caused by the porch, with its wooden pillars and tiled roof projection, falling down. The next shock would destroy the house, maybe. That rumble as of thunder was approaching again. The general was rushing round the room, to find the door, perhaps. He made a noise as though he were trying to climb the walls, and I heard him distinctly invoke the names of several saints. ' Out, out, Santierra! ' he yelled.

" The girl's voice was the only one I did not hear.

" ' General,' I cried, ' I cannot move the door. We must be locked in.'

" I did not recognise his voice in the shout of malediction and despair he let out. Señores, I know many men in my country, especially in the provinces most subject to earthquakes, who will neither eat, sleep, pray, nor even sit down to cards with closed doors. The danger is not in the loss of time, but in this—that the movement of the walls may prevent a door being opened at all. This was what had happened to us. We were trapped, and we had no help to expect from anybody. There is no man in my country who will go into a house when the earth trembles. There never was—except one: Gaspar Ruiz.

" He had come out of whatever hole he had been hiding in outside, and had clambered over the timbers of the destroyed porch. Above the awful subterranean groan of coming destruction I heard a mighty voice shouting the word ' Erminia! ' with the lungs of a giant. An earthquake is a great leveller of distinctions. I collected all my resolution against the terror of the scene. ' She is here,' I shouted back. A roar as of a furious wild beast answered me—while my head swam, my heart sank, and the sweat of anguish streamed like rain off my brow.

" He had the strength to pick up one of the heavy posts of the porch. Holding it under his armpit like a lance, but with both hands, he charged madly the rocking house with the force of a battering-ram, bursting open the door and rushing in, headlong, over our prostrate bodies. I and the general, picking ourselves up, bolted out together, without looking round once till we got across the road. Then, clinging to each other, we beheld the house change suddenly into a heap of formless rubbish behind the back of a man, who staggered towards us bearing the form of a woman clasped in his arms. Her long black hair hung nearly to his feet. He laid her down reverently on the heaving earth, and the moon-light shone on her closed eyes.

" Señores, we mounted with difficulty. Our horses, getting up, plunged madly, held by the soldiers who had come running from all sides. Nobody thought of catching Gaspar Ruiz then. The eyes of men and animals shone with wild fear. My general approached Gaspar Ruiz, who stood motionless as a statue above the girl. He let himself be shaken by the shoulder without detaching his eyes from her face.

" ' *Que guape !* ' shouted the general in his ear. ' You are the bravest man living. You have saved my life. I am General Robles. Come to my quarters to-morrow, if God gives us the grace to see another day.'

" He never stirred—as if deaf, without feeling, insensible.

" We rode away for the town, full of our rela-tions, of our friends, of whose fate we hardly dared to think. The soldiers ran by the side of our horses. Everything was forgotten in the immensity of the catastrophe overtaking a whole country."

*   *   *   *   *   *   *   *

Gaspar Ruiz saw the girl open her eyes. The raising of her eyelids seemed to recall him from a trance. They were alone; the cries of terror and distress from homeless people filled the plains of the coast, remote and immense, coming like a whisper into their loneliness.

She rose swiftly to her feet, darting fearful glances on all sides. " What is it? " she cried out low, and peering into his face. " Where am I? "

He bowed his head sadly, without a word.

" . . . Who are you? "

He knelt down slowly before her, and touched the hem of her coarse black baize skirt. " Your slave," he said.

She caught sight then of the heap of rubbish that had been the house, all misty in the cloud of dust. " Ah! " she cried, pressing her hand to her forehead.

" I carried you out from there," he whispered at her feet.

" And they? " she asked in a great sob.

He rose, and taking her by the arms, led her gently towards the shapeless ruin half over-whelmed by a land-slide. " Come and listen," he said.

The serene moon saw them clambering over that heap of stones, joists and tiles, which was a grave. They pressed their ears to the inter-stices, listening for the sound of a groan, for a sigh of pain.

At last he said, " They died swiftly. You are alone."

She sat down on a piece of broken timber and put one arm across her face. He waited—then, approaching his lips to her ear, " Let us go," he whispered.

" Never—never from here," she cried out, flinging her arms above her head.

He stooped over her, and her raised arms fell upon his shoulders. He lifted her up, steadied himself and began to walk, looking straight before him.

" What are you doing? " she asked feebly.

" I am escaping from my enemies," he said, never once glancing at his light burden.

" With me? " she sighed helplessly.

" Never without you," he said. " You are my strength."

He pressed her close to him. His face was grave and his footsteps steady. The conflagrations bursting out in the ruins of destroyed villages dotted the plain with red fires; and the sounds of distant lamentations, the cries of *" Misericordia! Misericordia! "* made a desolate murmur in his ears. He walked on, solemn and collected, as if carrying something holy, fragile and precious.

The earth rocked at times under his feet.

IX

WITH movements of mechanical care and an air of abstraction old General Santierra lighted a long and thick cigar.

"It was a good many hours before we could send a party back to the ravine," he said to his guests. "We had found one-third of the town laid low, the rest shaken up; and the inhabitants, rich and poor, reduced to the same state of distraction by the universal disaster. The affected cheerfulness of some contrasted with the despair of others. In the general confusion a number of reckless thieves, without fear of God or man, became a danger to those who from the downfall of their homes had managed to save some valuables. Crying ' *Misericordia* ' louder than any at every tremor, and beating their breasts with one hand, these scoundrels robbed the poor victims with the other, not even stopping short of murder.

"General Robles' division was occupied entirely in guarding the destroyed quarters of the town from the depredations of these inhuman monsters. Taken up with my duties of orderly officer, it was only in the morning that I could assure myself of the safety of my own family.

My mother and my sisters had escaped with
their lives from that ball-room, where I had left
them early in the evening. I remember those
two beautiful young women—God rest their souls
—as if I saw them this moment, in the garden of
our destroyed house, pale but active, assisting
some of our poor neighbours, in their soiled ball-
dresses and with the dust of fallen walls on their
hair. As to my mother, she had a stoical soul
in her frail body. Half-covered by a costly
shawl, she was lying on a rustic seat by the side
of an ornamental basin whose fountain had
ceased to play for ever on that night.

" I had hardly had time to embrace them all
with transports of joy, when my chief, coming
along, dispatched me to the ravine with a few
soldiers, to bring in my strong man, as he called
him, and that pale girl.

" But there was no one for us to bring in. A
land-slide had covered the ruins of the house;
and it was like a large mound of earth with only
the ends of some timbers visible here and there
—nothing more.

" Thus were the tribulations of the old Royalist
couple ended. An enormous and unconsecrated
grave had swallowed them up alive, in their unhappy obstinacy against the will of a people to
be free. And their daughter was gone.

" That Gaspar Ruiz had carried her off I understood very well. But as the case was not foreseen, I had no instructions to pursue them. And certainly I had no desire to do so. I had grown mistrustful of my interference. It had never been successful, and had not even appeared creditable. He was gone. Well, let him go. And he had carried off the Royalist girl! Nothing better. *Vaya con Dios*. This was not the time to bother about a deserter who, justly or unjustly, ought to have been dead, and a girl for whom it would have been better to have never been born.

" So I marched my men back to the town.

" After a few days, order having been re-established, all the principal families, including my own, left for Santiago. We had a fine house there. At the same time the division of Robles was moved to new cantonments near the capital. This change suited very well the state of my domestic and amorous feelings.

" One night, rather late, I was called to my chief. I found General Robles in his quarters, at ease, with his uniform off, drinking neat brandy out of a tumbler—as a precaution, he used to say, against the sleeplessness induced by the bites of mosquitoes. He was a good soldier, and he taught me the art and practice of war.

No doubt God has been merciful to his soul; for
his motives were never other than patriotic, if
his character was irascible. As to the use of
mosquito nets, he considered it effeminate, shame-
ful—unworthy of a soldier.

"I noticed at the first glance that his face,
already very red, wore an expression of high
good-humour.

"'Aha! *señor teniente*,' he cried loudly, as I
saluted at the door. 'Behold! Your strong man
has turned up again.'

"He extended to me a folded letter, which I
saw was superscribed 'To the Commander-in-
Chief of the Republican Armies.'

"'This,' General Robles went on in his loud
voice, 'was thrust by a boy into the hand of a
sentry at the *Quartel General*, while the fellow
stood there thinking of his girl, no doubt—for
before he could gather his wits together, the boy
had disappeared amongst the market people, and he
protests he could not recognise him to save his life.'

"My chief told me further that the soldier
had given the letter to the sergeant of the guard,
and that ultimately it had reached the hands of
our generalissimo. His Excellency had deigned
to take cognisance of it with his own eyes. After
that he had referred the matter in confidence to
General Robles.

" The letter, señores, I cannot now recollect textually. I saw the signature of Gaspar Ruiz. He was an audacious fellow. He had snatched a soul for himself out of a cataclysm, remember. And now it was that soul which had dictated the terms of his letter. Its tone was very independent. I remember it struck me at the time as noble—dignified. It was, no doubt, her letter. Now I shudder at the depth of its duplicity. Gaspar Ruiz was made to complain of the injustice of which he had been a victim. He invoked his previous record of fidelity and courage. Having been saved from death by the miraculous interposition of Providence, he could think of nothing but of retrieving his character. This, he wrote, he could not hope to do in the ranks as a discredited soldier still under suspicion. He had the means to give a striking proof of his fidelity. And he ended by proposing to the General-in-Chief a meeting at midnight in the middle of the Plaza before the Moneta. The signal would be to strike fire with flint and steel three times, which was not too conspicuous and yet distinctive enough for recognition.

" San Martin, the great Liberator, loved men of audacity and courage. Besides, he was just and compassionate. I told him as much of the man's story as I knew, and was ordered to accompany

him on the appointed night. The signals were
duly exchanged. It was midnight, and the whole
town was dark and silent. Their two cloaked
figures came together in the centre of the vast
Plaza, and, keeping discreetly at a distance, I
listened for an hour or more to the murmur of
their voices. Then the general motioned me to
approach; and as I did so I heard San Martin,
who was courteous to gentle and simple alike,
offer Gaspar Ruiz the hospitality of the headquarters for the night. But the soldier refused,
saying that he would not be worthy of that
honour till he had done something.

"'You cannot have a common deserter for
your guest, Excellency,' he protested with a low
laugh, and stepping backwards, merged slowly
into the night.

"The Commander-in-Chief observed to me, as
we turned away: 'He had somebody with him,
our friend Ruiz. I saw two figures for a moment.
It was an unobtrusive companion.'

"I too had observed another figure join the
vanishing form of Gaspar Ruiz. It had the appearance of a short fellow in a poncho and a big
hat. And I wondered stupidly who it could be
he had dared take into his confidence. I might
have guessed it could be no one but that fatal
girl—alas!

" Where he kept her concealed I do not know.
He had—it was known afterwards—an uncle, his
mother's brother, a small shopkeeper in Santiago.
Perhaps it was there that she found a roof and
food. Whatever she found, it was poor enough
to exasperate her pride and keep up her anger
and hate. It is certain she did not accompany
him on the feat he undertook to accomplish first
of all. It was nothing less than the destruction
of a store of war material collected secretly by
the Spanish authorities in the south, in a town
called Linares. Gaspar Ruiz was entrusted with
a small party only, but they proved themselves
worthy of San Martin's confidence. The season
was not propitious. They had to swim swollen
rivers. They seemed, however, to have galloped
night and day, outriding the news of their foray,
and holding straight for the town, a hundred
miles into the enemy's country, till at break of
day they rode into it sword in hand, surprising
the little garrison. It fled without making a
stand, leaving most of its officers in Gaspar Ruiz'
hands.

" A great explosion of gunpowder ended the
conflagration of the magazines the raiders had set
on fire without loss of time. In less than six
hours they were riding away at the same mad
speed, without the loss of a single man. Good as

they were, such an exploit is not performed
without a still better leadership.

"I was dining at the headquarters when Gaspar Ruiz himself brought the news of his success.
And it was a great blow to the Royalist troops.
For a proof he displayed to us the garrison's flag.
He took it from under his poncho and flung it on
the table. The man was transfigured; there was
something exulting and menacing in the expression of his face. He stood behind General San
Martin's chair and looked proudly at us all. He
had a round blue cap edged with silver braid on
his head, and we all could see a large white scar
on the nape of his sunburnt neck.

"Somebody asked him what he had done with
the captured Spanish officers.

"He shrugged his shoulders scornfully. 'What
a question to ask! In a partisan war you do not
burden yourself with prisoners. I let them go—
and here are their sword-knots.'

"He flung a bunch of them on the table upon
the flag. Then General Robles, whom I was attending there, spoke up in his loud, thick voice:
'You did! Then, my brave friend, you do not
know yet how a war like ours ought to be con-
ducted. You should have done—this.' And he
passed the edge of his hand across his own throat.

"Alas, señores! It was only too true that on

both sides this contest, in its nature so heroic, was stained by ferocity. The murmurs that arose at General Robles' words were by no means un- animous in tone. But the generous and brave San Martin praised the humane action, and pointed out to Ruiz a place on his right hand. Then rising with a full glass he proposed a toast: ' *Caballeros* and comrades-in-arms, let us drink the health of Captain Gaspar Ruiz.' And when we had emptied our glasses: ' I intend,' the Com- mander-in-Chief continued, ' to entrust him with the guardianship of our southern frontier, while we go afar to liberate our brethren in Peru. He whom the enemy could not stop from striking a blow at his very heart will know how to protect the peaceful populations we leave behind us to pursue our sacred task.' And he embraced the silent Gaspar Ruiz by his side.

" Later on, when we all rose from table, I ap- proached the latest officer of the army with my congratulations. ' And, Captain Ruiz,' I added, ' perhaps you do not mind telling a man who has always believed in the uprightness of your char- acter, what became of Doña Erminia on that night? '

" At this friendly question his aspect changed. He looked at me from under his eyebrows with the heavy, dull glance of a *guasso*—of a peasant.

E

'*Señor teniente,*' he said thickly, and as if very much cast down, 'do not ask me about the señorita, for I prefer not to think about her at all when I am amongst you.'

"He looked, with a frown, all about the room, full of smoking and talking officers. Of course I did not insist.

"These, señores, were the last words I was to hear him utter for a long, long time. The very next day we embarked for our arduous expedition to Peru, and we only heard of Gaspar Ruiz' doings in the midst of battles of our own. He had been appointed military guardian of our southern province. He raised a *partida*. But his leniency to the conquered foe displeased the Civil Governor, who was a formal, uneasy man, full of suspicions. He forwarded reports against Gaspar Ruiz to the Supreme Government; one of them being that he had married publicly, with great pomp, a woman of Royalist tendencies. Quarrels were sure to arise between these two men of very different character. At last the Civil Governor began to complain of his inactivity, and to hint at treachery, which, he wrote, would be not surprising in a man of such antecedents. Gaspar Ruiz heard of it. His rage flamed up, and the woman ever by his side knew how to feed it with perfidious words. I do not know whether really the Supreme Government ever did—as he complained afterwards—send orders for his arrest. It seems certain that the Civil Governor began to tamper with his officers, and that Gaspar Ruiz discovered the fact.

" One evening, when the Governor was giving a *tertullia*, Gaspar Ruiz, followed by six men he could trust, appeared riding through the town to the door of the Government House, and entered the *sala* armed, his hat on his head. As the Governor, displeased, advanced to meet him, he seized the wretched man round the body, carried him off from the midst of the appalled guests, as though he were a child, and flung him down the outer steps into the street. An angry hug from Gaspar Ruiz was enough to crush the life out of a giant; but in addition Gaspar Ruiz' horsemen fired their pistols at the body of the Governor as it lay motionless at the bottom of the stairs.

X

" AFTER this—as he called it—act of justice, Ruiz crossed the Rio Blanco, followed by the greater part of his band, and entrenched himself upon a hill. A company of regular troops sent out foolishly against him was surrounded, and destroyed almost to a man. Other expeditions, though better organised, were equally unsuccessful.

" It was during these sanguinary skirmishes that his wife first began to appear on horseback at his right hand. Rendered proud and self-confident by his successes, Ruiz no longer charged at the head of his *partida*, but presumptuously, like a general directing the movements of an army, he remained in the rear, well mounted and motionless on an eminence, sending out his orders. She was seen repeatedly at his side, and for a long time was mistaken for a man. There was much talk then of a mysterious white-faced chief, to whom the defeats of our troops were ascribed. She rode like an Indian woman, astride, wearing a broad-rimmed man's hat and a dark poncho. Afterwards, in the day of their greatest prosperity, this poncho was embroidered in gold, and she wore then, also, the sword of poor Don Antonio de Leyva. This veteran Chilian officer, having the misfortune to be surrounded with his small force, and running short of ammunition, found his death at the hands of the Arauco Indians, the allies and auxiliaries of Gaspar Ruiz. This was the fatal affair long remembered afterwards as the ' Massacre of the Island.' The sword of the unhappy officer was presented to her by

Peneleo, the Araucanian chief; for these Indians, struck by her aspect, the deathly pallor of her face, which no exposure to the weather seemed to affect, and her calm indifference under fire, looked upon her as a supernatural being, or at least as a witch. By this superstition the prestige and authority of Gaspar Ruiz amongst these ignorant people were greatly augmented. She must have savoured her vengeance to the full on that day when she buckled on the sword of Don Antonio de Leyva. It never left her side, unless she put on her woman's clothes—not that she would or could ever use it, but she loved to feel it beating upon her thigh as a perpetual reminder and symbol of the dishonour to the arms of the Republic. She was insatiable. Moreover, on the path she had led Gaspar Ruiz upon, there is no stopping. Escaped prisoners—and they were not many— used to relate how with a few whispered words she could change the expression of his face and revive his flagging animosity. They told how after every skirmish, after every raid, after every successful action, he would ride up to her and look into her face. Its haughty calm was never relaxed. Her embrace, señores, must have been as cold as the embrace of a statue. He tried to melt her icy heart in a stream of warm blood. Some English naval officers who visited him at that time noticed the strange character of his infatuation."

At the movement of surprise and curiosity in his audience General Santierra paused for a moment.

" Yes—English naval officers," he repeated. " Ruiz had consented to receive them to arrange for the liberation of some prisoners of your nationality.   In the territory upon which he ranged, from sea coast to the Cordillera, there was a bay where the ships of that time, after rounding Cape Horn, used to resort for wood and water. There, decoying the crew on shore, he captured first the whaling brig *Hersalia*, and afterwards made himself master by surprise of two more ships, one English and one American.

" It was rumoured at the time that he dreamed of setting up a navy of his own.   But that, of course, was impossible.   Still, manning the brig with part of her own crew, and putting an officer and a good many men of his own on board, he sent her off to the Spanish Governor of the island of Chiloe with a report of his exploits, and a demand for assistance in the war against the rebels.   The Governor could not do much for him; but he sent in return two light field-pieces, a letter of compliments, with a colonel's commission in the royal forces, and a great Spanish flag.   This standard with much ceremony was hoisted over his house in the heart of the Arauco country. Surely on that day she may have smiled on her *guasso* husband with a less haughty reserve.

" The senior officer of the English squadron on our coast made representations to our Government as to these captures. But Gaspar Ruiz refused to treat with us. Then an English frigate proceeded to the bay, and her captain, doctor, and two lieutenants travelled inland under a safe-conduct. They were well received, and spent three days as guests of the partisan chief. A sort of military, barbaric state was kept up at the residence. It was furnished with the loot of frontier towns. When first admitted to the principal *sala*, they saw his wife lying down (she was not in good health then), with Gaspar Ruiz sitting at the foot of the couch. His hat was lying on the floor, and his hands reposed on the hilt of his sword.

" During that first conversation he never removed his big hands from the sword-hilt, except once, to arrange the coverings about her, with gentle, careful touches. They noticed that whenever she spoke he would fix his eyes upon her in a kind of expectant, breathless attention, and seemingly forget the existence of the world and his own existence too. In the course of the fare-

well banquet, at which she was present reclining
on her couch, he burst forth into complaints of
the treatment he had received. After General
San Martin's departure he had been beset by
spies, slandered by civil officials, his services
ignored, his liberty and even his life threatened
by the Chilian Government. He got up from the
table, thundered execrations pacing the room
wildly, then sat down on the couch at his wife's
feet, his breast heaving, his eyes fixed on the
floor. She reclined on her back, her head on the
cushions, her eyes nearly closed.

" ' And now I am an honoured Spanish officer,'
he added in a calm voice.

" The captain of the English frigate then took
the opportunity to inform him gently that Lima
had fallen, and that by the terms of a convention
the Spaniards were withdrawing from the whole
continent.

" Gaspar Ruiz raised his head, and without
hesitation, speaking with suppressed vehemence,
declared that if not a single Spanish soldier were
left in the whole of South America he would per-
sist in carrying on the contest against Chile to
the last drop of blood. When he finished that mad
tirade his wife's long white hand was raised, and
she just caressed his knee with the tips of her
fingers for a fraction of a second.

" For the rest of the officers' stay, which did not extend for more than half an hour after the banquet, that ferocious chieftain of a desperate *partida* overflowed with amiability and kindness. He had been hospitable before, but now it seemed as though he could not do enough for the comfort and safety of his visitors' journey back to their ship.

" Nothing, I have been told, could have presented a greater contrast to his late violence or the habitual taciturn reserve of his manner. Like a man elated beyond measure by an unexpected happiness, he overflowed with good-will, amiability, and attentions. He embraced the officers like brothers, almost with tears in his eyes. The released prisoners were presented each with a piece of gold. At the last moment, suddenly, he declared he could do no less than restore to the masters of the merchant vessels all their private property. This unexpected generosity caused some delay in the departure of the party, and their first march was very short.

" Late in the evening Gaspar Ruiz rode up with an escort, to their camp fires, bringing along with him a mule loaded with cases of wine. He had come, he said, to drink a stirrup cup with his English friends, whom he would never see again. He was mellow and joyous in his temper. He

*E

told stories of his own exploits, laughed like a
boy, borrowed a guitar from the Englishmen's
chief muleteer, and sitting cross-legged on his
superfine poncho spread before the glow of the
embers, sang a *guasso* love-song in a tender voice.
Then his head dropped on his breast, his hands
fell to the ground; the guitar rolled off his knees
—and a great hush fell over the camp after the
love-song of the implacable partisan who had
made so many of our people weep for destroyed
homes and for loves cut short.

" Before anybody could make a sound he
sprang up from the ground and called for his
horse.

" ' *Adios*, my friends! ' he cried. ' Go with
God. I love you. And tell them well in Santiago
that between Gaspar Ruiz, colonel of the King of
Spain, and the republican carrion-crows of Chile
there is war to the last breath—war! war! war! '

" With a great yell of ' War! war! war! '
which his escort took up, they rode away, and the
sound of hoofs and of voices died out in the distance between the slopes of the hills.

" The two young English officers were convinced that Ruiz was mad. How do you say
that?—tile loose—eh? But the doctor, an obser-
vant Scotsman with much shrewdness and philo-
sophy in his character, told me that it was a very

curious case of possession. I met him many years afterwards, but he remembered the experience very well. He told me too that in his opinion that woman did not lead Gaspar Ruiz into the practice of sanguinary treachery by direct persuasion, but by the subtle way of awakening and keeping alive in his simple mind a burning sense of an irreparable wrong. Maybe, maybe. But I would say that she poured half of her vengeful soul into the strong clay of that man, as you may pour intoxication, madness, poison into an empty cup.

" If he wanted war he got it in earnest when our victorious army began to return from Peru. Systematic operations were planned against this blot on the honour and prosperity of our hardly-won independence. General Robles commanded, with his well-known ruthless severity. Savage reprisals were exercised on both sides, and no quarter was given in the field. Having won my promotion in the Peru campaign, I was a captain on the staff.

" Gaspar Ruiz found himself hard pressed; at the same time we heard by means of a fugitive priest who had been carried off from his village presbytery, and galloped eighty miles into the hills to perform the christening ceremony, that a daughter was born to them. To celebrate the event, I suppose, Ruiz executed one or two brilliant forays clear away at the rear of our forces, and defeated the detachments sent out to cut off his retreat. General Robles nearly had a stroke of apoplexy from rage. He found another cause of insomnia than the bites of mosquitoes; but against this one, señores, tumblers of raw brandy had no more effect than so much water. He took to railing and storming at me about my strong man. And from our impatience to end this inglorious campaign, I am afraid that we young officers became reckless and apt to take undue risks on service.

" Nevertheless, slowly, inch by inch as it were, our columns were closing upon Gaspar Ruiz, though he had managed to raise all the Araucanian nation of wild Indians against us. Then a year or more later our Government became aware through its agents and spies that he had actually entered into alliance with Carreras, the so-called dictator of the so-called republic of Mendoza, on the other side of the mountains. Whether Gaspar Ruiz had a deep political intention, or whether he wished only to secure a safe retreat for his wife and child while he pursued remorselessly against us his war of surprises and massacres, I cannot tell. The alliance, however, was a fact. Defeated in his attempt to check our advance from the sea, he retreated with his usual swiftness, and preparing for another hard and hazardous tussle, began by sending his wife with the little girl across the Pequeña range of mountains, on the frontier of Mendoza.

XI

" Now Carreras, under the guise of politics and liberalism, was a scoundrel of the deepest dye, and the unhappy state of Mendoza was the prey of thieves, robbers, traitors and murderers, who formed his party. He was under a noble exterior a man without heart, pity, honour, or conscience. He aspired to nothing but tyranny, and though he would have made use of Gaspar Ruiz for his nefarious designs, yet he soon became aware that to propitiate the Chilian Government would answer his purpose better. I blush to say that he made proposals to our Government to deliver up on certain conditions the wife and child of the man who had trusted to his honour, and that this offer was accepted.

" While on her way to Mendoza over the Pequeña pass she was betrayed by her escort of Carreras' men, and given up to the officer in command of a Chilian fort on the upland at the foot

of the main Cordillera range.   This atrocious
transaction might have cost me dear, for as a
matter of fact I was a prisoner in Gaspar Ruiz'
camp when he received the news.   I had been
captured during a reconnaissance, my escort of a
few troopers being speared by the Indians of his
bodyguard.   I was saved from the same fate
because he recognised my features just in time.
No doubt my friends thought I was dead, and I
would not have given much for my life at any
time.   But the strong man treated me very well,
because, he said, I had always believed in his
innocence and had tried to serve him when he
was a victim of injustice.

"'And now,' was his speech to me, 'you shall
see that I always speak the truth.   You are safe.'

"I did not think I was very safe when I was
called up to go to him one night.   He paced up
and down like a wild beast, exclaiming, 'Betrayed!   Betrayed!'

"He walked up to me clenching his fists.   'I
could cut your throat.'

"'Will that give your wife back to you?' I
said as quietly as I could.

"'And the child!' he yelled out, as if mad.
He fell into a chair and laughed in a frightful,
boisterous manner.   'Oh, no, you are safe.'

"I assured him that his wife's life was safe

too; but I did not say what I was convinced of
—that he would never see her again. He wanted
war to the death, and the war could only end with
his death.

" He gave me a strange, inexplicable look, and
sat muttering blankly, ' In their hands. In their
hands.'

" I kept as still as a mouse before a cat.

" Suddenly he jumped up. ' What am I doing
here? ' he cried; and opening the door, he yelled
out orders to saddle and mount. ' What is it? '
he stammered, coming up to me. ' The Pequeña
fort; a fort of palisades! Nothing. I would get
her back if she were hidden in the very heart of
the mountain.' He amazed me by adding, with
an effort: ' I carried her off in my two arms while
the earth trembled. And the child at least is
mine. She at least is mine! '

" Those were bizarre words; but I had no time
for wonder.

" ' You shall go with me,' he said violently. ' I
may want to parley, and any other messenger
from Ruiz, the outlaw, would have his throat
cut.'

" This was true enough. Between him and the
rest of incensed mankind there could be no communication, according to the customs of honour-
able warfare.

" In less than half an hour we were in the saddle, flying wildly through the night. He had only an escort of twenty men at his quarters, but would not wait for more. He sent, however, messengers to Peneleo, the Indian chief then ranging in the foothills, directing him to bring his warriors to the uplands and meet him at the lake called the Eye of Water, near whose shores the frontier fort of Pequeña was built.

" We crossed the lowlands with that untired rapidity of movement which had made Gaspar Ruiz' raids so famous. We followed the lower valleys up to their precipitous heads. The ride was not without its dangers. A cornice road on a perpendicular wall of basalt wound itself around a buttressing rock, and at last we emerged from the gloom of a deep gorge upon the upland of Pequeña.

" It was a plain of green wiry grass and thin flowering bushes; but high above our heads patches of snow hung in the folds and crevices of the great walls of rock. The little lake was as round as a staring eye. The garrison of the fort were just driving in their small herd of cattle when we appeared. Then the great wooden gates swung to, and that four-square enclosure of broad blackened stakes pointed at the top and barely hiding the grass roofs of the huts inside, seemed deserted, empty, without a single soul.

"But when summoned to surrender, by a man who at Gaspar Ruiz' order rode fearlessly forward, those inside answered by a volley which rolled him and his horse over. I heard Ruiz by my side grind his teeth. 'It does not matter,' he said. 'Now you go.'

"Torn and faded as its rags were, the vestiges of my uniform were recognised, and I was allowed to approach within speaking distance; and then I had to wait, because a voice clamouring through a loophole with joy and astonishment would not allow me to place a word. It was the voice of Major Pajol, an old friend. He, like my other comrades, had thought me killed a long time ago.

"'Put spurs to your horse, man!' he yelled, in the greatest excitement; 'we will swing the gate open for you.'

"I let the reins fall out of my hand and shook my head. 'I am on my honour,' I cried.

"'To him!' he shouted, with infinite disgust.

"'He promises you your life.'

"'Our life is our own. And do you, Santierra, advise us to surrender to that *rastrero*?'

"'No!' I shouted. 'But he wants his wife and child, and he can cut you off from water.'

" ' Then she would be the first to suffer. You may tell him that. Look here—this is all nonsense: we shall dash out and capture you.'

" ' You shall not catch me alive,' I said firmly.

" ' Imbecile! '

" ' For God's sake,' I continued hastily, ' do not open the gate.' And I pointed at the multitude of Peneleo's Indians who covered the shores of the lake.

" I had never seen so many of these savages together. Their lances seemed as numerous as stalks of grass. Their hoarse voices made a vast, inarticulate sound like the murmur of the sea.

" My friend Pajol was swearing to himself. ' Well, then—go to the devil! ' he shouted, exasperated. But as I swung round he repented, for I heard him say hurriedly, ' Shoot the fool's horse before he gets away.'

" He had good marksmen. Two shots rang out, and in the very act of turning my horse staggered, fell and lay still as if struck by lightning. I had my feet out of the stirrups and rolled clear of him; but I did not attempt to rise. Neither dared they rush out to drag me in.

" The masses of Indians had begun to move upon the fort. They rode up in squadrons, trailing their long *chusos*; then dismounted out of musket-shot, and, throwing off their fur mantles,

advanced naked to the attack, stamping their feet
and shouting in cadence. A sheet of flame ran
three times along the face of the fort without
checking their steady march. They crowded right
up to the very stakes, flourishing their broad
knives. But this palisade was not fastened together with hide lashings in the usual way, but
with long iron nails, which they could not cut.
Dismayed at the failure of their usual method
of forcing an entrance, the heathen, who had
marched so steadily against the musketry fire,
broke and fled under the volleys of the besieged.

" Directly they had passed me on their advance
I got up and rejoined Gaspar Ruiz on a low ridge
which jutted out upon the plain. The musketry
of his own men had covered the attack, but now
at a sign from him a trumpet sounded the ' Cease
fire.' Together we looked in silence at the hope-
less rout of the savages.

" ' It must be a siege, then,' he muttered. And
I detected him wringing his hands stealthily.

" But what sort of siege could it be? Without
any need for me to repeat my friend Pajol's
message, he dared not cut the water off from the
besieged. They had plenty of meat. And, indeed,
if they had been short, he would have been too
anxious to send food into the stockade had he
been able. But, as a matter of fact, it was we on

the plain who were beginning to feel the pinch of hunger.

" Peneleo, the Indian chief, sat by our fire folded in his ample mantle of guanaco skins. He was an athletic savage, with an enormous square shock head of hair resembling a straw beehive in shape and size, and with grave, surly, much-lined features. In his broken Spanish he repeated, growling like a bad-tempered wild beast, that if an opening ever so small were made in the stockade his men would march in and get the señora —not otherwise.

" Gaspar Ruiz, sitting opposite him, kept his eyes fixed on the fort night and day as it were, in awful silence and immobility. Meantime, by runners from the lowlands that arrived nearly every day, we heard of the defeat of one of his lieutenants in the Maipu valley. Scouts sent afar brought news of a column of infantry advancing through distant passes to the relief of the fort. They were slow, but we could trace their toilful progress up the lower valleys. I wondered why Ruiz did not march to attack and destroy this threatening force, in some wild gorge fit for an ambuscade, in accordance with his genius for guerilla warfare. But his genius seemed to have abandoned him to his despair.

" It was obvious to me that he could not tear

himself away from the sight of the fort. I protest to you, señores, that I was moved almost to pity by the sight of this powerless strong man sitting on the ridge, indifferent to sun, to rain, to cold, to wind; with his hands clasped round his legs and his chin resting on his knees, gazing—gazing —gazing.

" And the fort he kept his eyes fastened on was as still and silent as himself. The garrison gave no sign of life. They did not even answer the desultory fire directed at the loopholes.

" One night, as I strolled past him, he, without changing his attitude, spoke to me unexpectedly ' I have sent for a gun,' he said. ' I shall have time to get her back and retreat before your Robles manages to crawl up here.'

" He had sent for a gun to the plains.

" It was long in coming, but at last it came. It was a seven-pounder field-gun. Dismounted and lashed crosswise to two long poles, it had been carried up the narrow paths between two mules with ease. His wild cry of exultation at day-break when he saw the gun escort emerge from the valley rings in my ears now.

" But, señores, I have no words to depict his amazement, his fury, his despair and distraction, when he heard that the animal loaded with the gun-carriage had, during the last night march, somehow or other tumbled down a precipice. He broke into menaces of death and torture against the escort. I kept out of his way all that day, lying behind some bushes, and wondering what he would do now. Retreat was left for him; but he could not retreat.

" I saw below me his artillerist, Jorge, an old Spanish soldier, building up a sort of structure with heaped-up saddles. The gun, ready-loaded, was lifted on to that, but in the act of firing the whole thing collapsed and the shot flew high above the stockade.

" Nothing more was attempted. One of the ammunition mules had been lost too, and they had no more than six shots to fire; amply enough to batter down the gate, providing the gun was well laid. This was impossible without it being properly mounted. There was no time nor means to construct a carriage. Already every moment I expected to hear Robles' bugle-calls echo amongst the crags.

" Peneleo, wandering about uneasily, draped in his skins, sat down for a moment near me growling his usual tale.

" ' Make an *entrada*—a hole. If make a hole, *bueno*. If not make a hole, them *vamos*—we must go away.'

" After sunset I observed with surprise the

Indians making preparations as if for another
assault. Their lines stood ranged in the shadows
of the mountains. On the plain in front of the
fort gate I saw a group of men swaying about in
the same place.

" I walked down the ridge disregarded. The
moonlight in the clear air of the uplands was as
bright as day, but the intense shadows confused
my sight, and I could not make out what they
were doing. I heard the voice of Jorge, the
artillerist, say in a queer, doubtful tone, ' It is
loaded, señores.'

" Then another voice in that group pronounced
firmly the words, ' Bring the *riata* here.' It was
the voice of Gaspar Ruiz.

" A silence fell, in which the popping shots of
the besieged garrison rang out sharply. They too
had observed the group. But the distance was
too great, and in the spatter of spent musket-balls
cutting up the ground, the group opened, closed,
swayed, giving me a glimpse of busy stooping
figures in its midst. I drew nearer, doubting
whether this was a weird vision, a suggestive and
insensate dream.

" A strangely stifled voice commanded, ' Haul
the hitches tighter.'

" ' *Si, señor*,' several other voices answered in
tones of awed alacrity.

"Then the stifled voice said: 'Like this. I must be free to breathe.'

"Then there was a concerned noise of many men together. 'Help him up, *hombres*. Steady! Under the other arm.'

"That deadened voice ordered: '*Bueno !* Stand away from me, men.'

"I pushed my way through the recoiling circle, and heard once more that same oppressed voice saying earnestly: 'Forget that I am a living man, Jorge. Forget me altogether, and think of what you have to do.'

"'Be without fear, señor. You are nothing to me but a gun carriage, and I shall not waste a shot.'

"I heard the spluttering of a port-fire, and smelt the saltpetre of the match. I saw suddenly before me a nondescript shape on all fours like a beast, but with a man's head drooping below a tubular projection over the nape of the neck, and the gleam of a rounded mass of bronze on its back.

"In front of a silent semicircle of men it squatted alone with Jorge behind it and a trumpeter motionless, his trumpet in his hand, by its side.

"Jorge, bent double, muttered, port-fire in hand: 'An inch to the left, señor. Too much. So.

Now, if you let yourself down a little by letting
your elbows bend, I will . . .'

" He leaped aside, lowering his port-fire, and a
burst of flame darted out of the muzzle of the gun
lashed on the man's back.

" Then Gaspar Ruiz lowered himself slowly.
' Good shot? ' he asked.

" ' Full on, señor.'

" ' Then load again.'

" He lay there before me on his breast under
the darkly glittering bronze of his monstrous
burden, such as no love or strength of man had
ever had to bear in the lamentable history of the
world. His arms were spread out, and he resembled a prostrate penitent on the moonlit ground.

" Again I saw him raised to his hands and
knees, and the men stand away from him, and
old Jorge stoop, glancing along the gun.

" ' Left a little. Right an inch. *Por Dios, señor*,
stop this trembling. Where is your strength? '

" The old gunner's voice was cracked with
emotion. He stepped aside, and quick as lightning brought the spark to the touch-hole.

" ' Excellent! ' he cried tearfully; but Gaspar
Ruiz lay for a long time silent, flattened on the
ground.

" ' I am tired,' he murmured at last. ' Will
another shot do it? '

" ' Without doubt,' said Jorge, bending down to his ear.

" ' Then—load,' I heard him utter distinctly. ' Trumpeter!'

" ' I am here, señor, ready for your word.'

" ' Blow a blast at this word that shall be heard from one end of Chile to the other,' he said, in an extraordinarily strong voice. ' And you others stand ready to cut this accursed *riata*, for then will be the time for me to lead you in your rush. Now raise me up, and, you, Jorge—be quick with your aim.'

" The rattle of musketry from the fort nearly drowned his voice. The palisade was wreathed in smoke and flame.

" ' Exert your force forward against the recoil, *mi amo*,' said the old gunner shakily. ' Dig your fingers into the ground. So. Now!'

" A cry of exultation escaped him after the shot. The trumpeter raised his trumpet nearly to his lips, and waited. But no word came from the prostrate man. I fell on one knee, and heard all he had to say then.

" ' Something broken,' he whispered, lifting his head a little, and turning his eyes towards me in his hopelessly crushed attitude.

" ' The gate hangs only by the splinters,' yelled Jorge.

" Gaspar Ruiz tried to speak, but his voice died out in his throat, and I helped to roll the gun off his broken back. He was insensible.

" I kept my lips shut, of course. The signal for the Indians to attack was never given. Instead, the bugle-calls of the relieving force, for which my ears had thirsted so long, burst out, terrifying like the call of the Last Day to our surprised enemies.

" A tornado, señores, a real hurricane of stampeded men, wild horses, mounted Indians, swept over me as I cowered on the ground by the side of Gaspar Ruiz, still stretched out on his face in the shape of a cross. Peneleo, galloping for life, jabbed at me with his long *chuso* in passing—for the sake of old acquaintance, I suppose. How I escaped the flying lead is more difficult to explain. Venturing to rise on my knees too soon, some soldiers of the 17th Taltal regiment, in their hurry to get at something alive, nearly bayonetted me on the spot. They looked very disappointed too when some officers galloping up drove them away with the flat of their swords.

" It was General Robles with his staff. He wanted badly to make some prisoners. He, too, seemed disappointed for a moment. ' What? Is it you? ' he cried. But he dismounted at once to embrace me, for he was an old friend of my

family. I pointed to the body at our feet, and
said only these two words:

"'Gaspar Ruiz.'

"He threw his arms up in astonishment.

"'Aha! Your strong man! Always to the last
with your strong man. No matter. He saved our
lives when the earth trembled enough to make the
bravest faint with fear. I was frightened out of
my wits. But he—no! *Que guape!* Where's the
hero who got the best of him? Ha! ha! ha!
What killed him, *chico*?'

"'His own strength, general,' I answered.

XII

"But Gaspar Ruiz breathed yet. I had him
carried in his poncho under the shelter of some
bushes on the very ridge from which he had been
gazing so fixedly at the fort while unseen death
was hovering already over his head.

"Our troops had bivouacked round the fort.
Towards daybreak I was not surprised to hear
that I was designated to command the escort of a
prisoner who was to be sent down at once to
Santiago. Of course the prisoner was Gaspar
Ruiz' wife.

" ' I have named you out of regard for your feelings,' General Robles remarked. ' Though the woman really ought to be shot for all the harm she has done to the Republic.'

" And as I made a movement of shocked protest, he continued:

" ' Now he is as well as dead, she is of no importance. Nobody will know what to do with her. However, the Government wants her.' He shrugged his shoulders. ' I suppose he must have buried large quantities of his loot in places that she alone knows of.'

" At dawn I saw her coming up the ridge, guarded by two soldiers, and carrying her child on her arm.

" I walked to meet her.

" ' Is he living yet? ' she asked, confronting me with that white, impassive face he used to look at in an adoring way.

" I bent my head, and led her round a clump of bushes without a word. His eyes were open. He breathed with difficulty, and uttered her name with a great effort.

" ' Erminia! '

" She knelt at his head. The little girl, unconscious of him, and with her big eyes looking about, began to chatter suddenly, in a joyous, thin voice. She pointed a tiny finger at the rosy glow of sunrise behind the black shapes of the peaks. And while that child-talk, incomprehensible and sweet to the ear, lasted, those two, the dying man and the kneeling woman, remained silent, looking into each other's eyes, listening to the frail sound. Then the prattle stopped. The child laid its head against its mother's breast and was still.

" ' It was for you,' he began. ' Forgive.' His voice failed him. Presently I heard a mutter, and caught the pitiful words: ' Not strong enough.'

" She looked at him with an extraordinary intensity. He tried to smile, and in a humble tone, ' Forgive me,' he repeated. ' Leaving you . . .'

" She bent down, dry-eyed, and in a steady voice: ' On all the earth I have loved nothing but you, Gaspar,' she said.

" His head made a movement. His eyes revived. ' At last ! ' he sighed out. Then, anxiously, ' But is this true . . . is this true ? '

" ' As true as that there is no mercy and justice in this world,' she answered him passionately. She stooped over his face. He tried to raise his head, but it fell back, and when she kissed his lips he was already dead. His glazed eyes stared at the sky, on which pink clouds floated very high. But I noticed the eyelids of the child, pressed to its mother's breast, droop and close slowly. She had gone to sleep.

" The widow of Gaspar Ruiz, the strong man, allowed me to lead her away without shedding a tear.

" For travelling we had arranged for her a side-saddle very much like a chair, with a board swung beneath to rest her feet on. And the first day she rode without uttering a word, and hardly for one moment turning her eyes away from the little girl, whom she held on her knees. At our first camp I saw her during the night walking about, rocking the child in her arms and gazing down at it by the light of the moon. After we had started on our second day's march she asked me how soon we should come to the first village of the inhabited country.

" I said we should be there about noon.

" ' And will there be women there? ' she inquired.

" I told her that it was a large village. ' There will be men and women there, señora,' I said, ' whose hearts shall be made glad by the news that all the unrest and war is over now.'

" ' Yes, it is all over now,' she repeated. Then, after a time: ' Señor officer, what will your Government do with me? '

" ' I do not know, señora,' I said. ' They will

treat you well, no doubt We republicans are not savages, and take no vengeance on women.'

" She gave me a look at the word ' republicans ' which I imagined full of undying hate. But an hour or so afterwards, as we drew up to let the baggage mules go first along a narrow path skirting a precipice, she looked at me with such a white, troubled face that I felt a great pity for her.

" ' Señor officer,' she said, ' I am weak, I tremble. It is an insensate fear.' And indeed her lips did tremble, while she tried to smile glancing at the beginning of the narrow path which was not so dangerous after all. ' I am afraid I shall drop the child. Gaspar saved your life, you remember. . . . Take her from me.'

" I took the child out of her extended arms. ' Shut your eyes, señora, and trust to your mule,' I recommended.

" She did so, and with her pallor and her wasted thin face she looked deathlike. At a turn of the path, where a great crag of purple porphyry closes the view of the lowlands, I saw her open her eyes. I rode just behind her holding the little girl with my right arm. ' The child is all right,' I cried encouragingly.

" ' Yes,' she answered faintly; and then, to my intense terror, I saw her stand up on the footrest, staring horribly, and throw herself forward into the chasm on our right.

"I cannot describe to you the sudden and abject fear that came over me at that dreadful sight. It was a dread of the abyss, the dread of the crags which seemed to nod upon me. My head swam. I pressed the child to my side and sat my horse as still as a statue. I was speechless and cold all over. Her mule staggered, sidling close to the rock, and then went on. My horse only pricked up his ears with a slight snort. My heart stood still, and from the depths of the precipice the stones rattling in the bed of the furious stream made me almost insane with their sound.

"Next moment we were round the turn and on a broad and grassy slope. And then I yelled. My men came running back to me in great alarm. It seems that at first I did nothing but shout, ' She has given the child into my hands! She has given the child into my hands!' The escort thought I had gone mad."

General Santierra ceased and got up from the table. "And that is all, señores," he concluded, with a courteous glance at his rising guests.

"But what became of the child, General?" we asked.

"Ah, the child, the child."

F

He walked to one of the windows opening on his beautiful garden, the refuge of his old days. Its fame was great in the land. Keeping us back with a raised arm, he called out, " Erminia, Erminia! " and waited. Then his cautioning arm dropped, and we crowded to the windows.

From a clump of trees a woman had come upon the broad walk bordered with flowers. We could hear the rustle of her starched petticoats and observed the ample spread of her old-fashioned black silk skirt. She looked up, and seeing all these eyes staring at her, stopped, frowned, smiled, shook her finger at the General, who was laughing boisterously, and drawing the black lace on her head so as to partly conceal her haughty profile, passed out of our sight, walking with stiff dignity.

" You have beheld the guardian angel of the old man—and her to whom you owe all that is seemly and comfortable in my hospitality. Somehow, señores, though the flame of love has been kindled early in my breast, I have never married. And because of that perhaps the sparks of the sacred fire are not yet extinct here." He struck his broad chest. " Still alive, still alive," he said, with serio-comic emphasis. " But I shall not marry now. She is General Santierra's adopted daughter and heiress."

One of our fellow-guests, a young naval officer, described her afterwards as a " short, stout, old girl of forty or thereabouts." We had all noticed that her hair was turning grey, and that she had very fine black eyes.

" And," General Santierra continued, " neither would she ever hear of marrying any one. A real calamity! Good, patient, devoted to the old man. A simple soul. But I would not advise any of you to ask for her hand, for if she took yours into hers it would be only to crush your bones. Ah! she does not jest on that subject. And she is the own daughter of her father, the strong man who perished through his own strength: the strength of his body, of his simplicity—of his love! "

Youth was not my first contribution to " Maga " [1] It was the second. But that story marks the first appearance in the world of the man Marlow, with whom my relations have grown very intimate in the course of years. The origins of that gentleman (nobody as far as I know had ever hinted that he was anything but that)—his origins have been the subject of some literary speculation of, I am glad to say, a friendly nature.

One would think that I am the proper person to throw a light on the matter; but in truth I find that it isn't so easy. It is pleasant to remember that nobody had charged him with fraudulent purposes or looked down on him as a charlatan; but apart from that he was supposed to be all sorts of things: a clever screen, a mere device, a " personator," a familiar spirit, a whispering " dæmon." I myself have been suspected of a meditated plan for his capture.

That is not so. I made no plans. The man Marlow and I came together in the casual manner of those health-resort acquaintances which sometimes ripen into friendships. This one has ripened.

For all his assertiveness in matters of opinion he is not an intrusive person. He haunts my hours of solitude, when, in silence, we lay our heads together in great comfort and harmony; but as we part at the end of a tale I am never sure that it may not be for the last time. Yet I don't think that either of us would care much to survive the other. In his case, at any rate, his occupation would be gone and he would suffer from that extinction, because I suspect him of some vanity. I don't mean vanity in the Solomonian sense. Of all my people he's the one that has never been a vexation to my spirit. A most discreet, understanding man. . . .

Even before appearing in book form *Youth* was very well received. It lies on me to confess at last, and this is as good a place for it as another, that I have been all my life—all my two lives—the spoiled adopted child of Great Britain and even of the Empire; for it was Australia that gave me my first command. I break out into this declaration not because of a lurking tendency to megalomania, but, on the contrary, as a man who has no very notable illusions about himself. I follow the instincts of vainglory and humility natural to all mankind. For it can hardly be denied that it is not their own deserts that men are most proud of, but rather of their prodigious luck, of

their marvellous fortune: of that in their lives for
which thanks and sacrifices must be offered on
the altars of the inscrutable gods.

The story *Gaspar Ruiz* is not a piece of personal experience like *Youth*. It is truly fiction, by
which I do not mean that it is merely invented,
but that it is truly imagined from hints of things
that have really happened and of people that have
really existed at that time, in that locality and
under those special conditions of life. It can be
easily understood that for that sort of work, which
is of course of a creative (not reminiscent) nature,
a certain knowledge of the epoch, the outcome of
reading and mental assimilation, was necessary.
I need not say that such knowledge as I had was
used throughout with a scrupulous regard to the
truth of it. No incident was introduced arbi-
trarily but only as a necessary touch in the general
picture. In this arrangement consists the art of
story-telling as distinguished from the style. My
suggestion for *Gaspar Ruiz* I found in an old book
of travels published in 1830, both as to his personal appearance and as to certain facts and
adventures of his life. The real name of the man
was Benavides, and he was really for a time chief
of a band of Partisans during the Independence
War in South America, in the years 1822–24. He

did change sides, his wife *was* betrayed to one of his enemies, as in the story, together with his little girl, and his character really *was* audacious, ruthless and enterprising. He was really visited by the officers of a British man-of-war in reference to the release of some captured Englishmen. But all this information was contained in less than two full pages of the book. I had to imagine the motives of actions, the various states of people's minds, and the outward appearance of all the persons involved in the tale. Yet no incident or trait of character has been introduced for the sake of its mere sensational value, but only in order to give a true presentation of the feelings, perplexities and passions roused in human breasts by a sequence of certain events which, in the strictest truth, might have happened, and for the most part *did* actually happen, at that time and place.

The episode of the gun fired from the man's back is a reminiscence of my boyhood's reading. Much later in life I heard of it again as an undoubted fact. I am assured, that, supposing the gun to be an old brass four-pounder, taking into account the exceptional physique of Gaspar Ruiz and the use of such a comparatively mild explosive as the gunpowder of that time, it is not impossible.

A CONRAD CATECHISM

A CONRAD CATECHISM

The following Questions and Exercises, drawn up by Dr. Richard Wilson, were approved by the author in the spring of 1920.

I. YOUTH

1. Speaking from your own experience, how far do you assent to the truth of the first paragraph?

2. Consider the word-picture contained in the first sentence of the second paragraph.

3. What are mail-boats like at the present day?

4. The author uses words carefully. What is the real difference between a story and a chronicle?

5. Mark and memorise the sentence, "Voyages that seem ordered for the illustration of life, that might stand for a symbol of existence."

6. Consider the portrait of the skipper. Select one or two phrases of the description which you think more significant than others. Contrast this portrait with that of the first mate. Are the "two grandfathers" clearly distinct? Would you confuse either with Jermyn?

7. What kind of opinion have you formed of Marlowe's own character?

8. From the words "They loaded us at last" to "that fool of a steamer smashed" there is a series of pictures which pass with the speed of a film. Study the manner in which this effect is produced.

9. Draw up a time-table of this voyage to Bangkok.

10. Can you find the phrases which prove that the writer personifies the sou'-west wind? Read again and again the description of the tossing of the ship "like an old candle-box."

11. The paragraph beginning "O youth! The strength of it . . ." Can you think of an appropriate title for this passage?

12. Can you find a few occasional phrases which prevent the reader from forgetting Marlow's companions?

13. What is the refrain of this "chronicle"? (*N.B.*—The answer to this question is not "Pass the bottle.")

14. Quote a passage showing how the author personifies a ship.

15. Memorise the paragraph, "And for me there was also my youth . . . Do or die"; also the paragraph, ". . . The sky was a miracle . . . sea and sky."

16. Can you trace the route from Falmouth on a globe from the few hints here given?

17. Study carefully the magnificent description in the passage beginning "Next day it was my watch on deck . . . to take the wheel himself"; and the still more splendid picture of the departure of the steamer.

18. What was the effect of all the troubles upon (1) the Captain, (2) Mahon, (3) Marlow, (4) the seamen?

19. If you were an artist and were asked to illustrate that portion of the story which tells of the fire, what scene would you select?

20. The sinking of the ship is impressive. How would a melodramatic writer have described the last glimpse of her "creed and name"?

21. Comment upon the sentence, "He was a malicious old man—and may the deep sea where he sleeps now rock him gently, rock him tenderly to the end of time!"

22. Which sentence on page 56 recalls the fact that Marlow is telling a story to several other men?

23. Read aloud, and memorise, if you are interested, the paragraph, "And this is how I see the East . . . whispered promise of mysterious delight." The whole of this part of the "chronicle" is full of haunting beauty and the music of words.

24. Then upon the magic and romance breaks in—what? What effect has this interruption upon the feeling of the story? When does the comic element assert itself in a well-constructed play?

25. The climax is contained in the paragraph, "And then I saw the men of the East . . . Night —Good-bye . . .!" Read and re-read this glorious passage.

26. The picture in the polished table recurs at the end of the chronicle. The description is worthy of more than ordinary attention.

27. Write down your own frank opinion on the qualities of this chronicle. Beware of the phrases of ordinary criticism. Put your opinion in the form of a familiar letter to a friend telling him (or her) what you have been reading and what you think about it.

28. What do you consider the most humorous touches in the story?

29. Who (or what) is the hero (or heroine) of this story?

II. GASPAR RUIZ

1. Test the truth of the first two sentences in Section I by applying them to the Great War; also of the sentence, "As is usual in war, the mass of the people, who had the least to gain by the issue, suffered most in their obscure persons and their humble fortunes."

2. Look up Peru in an encyclopaedia and date the war referred to on page 70.

3. What is the author's opinion of war?

4. What historical incident is recalled by a portion of Section II?

5. Consider the remarks about proverbs in the first part of Section V in connection with the following:

(a) Honesty is the best policy.
(b) Wilful waste makes woeful want.

(c) A stitch in time saves nine.
(d) Early to bed and early to rise
    Makes a man healthy, wealthy, and wise.

6. Study the grim pictorial quality of the execution scene. Is there any suggestion of connection or sympathy between Nature and the doings of men?

7. Apart from the execution scene, what is the most striking picture of Section V—and its most striking phrase?

8. What is the most telling phrase in the first description of the old Spanish royalist in Section VI?

9. Would you call General Santierra a cynic?

10. Select a striking word - picture from Section VII.

11. The story is alternately related and reported. What is the effect of the change?

12. Consider carefully the deep meaning of the paragraph, "She crushed him with her glance. The power of her will to be understood was so strong that it kindled in him the intelligence of unexpressed things."

13. Can you find a sentence in Section VIII which might have been spoken by Nurse Cavell?

14. What do you consider the finest picture of Section VIII?

15. Consider the truth of the sentence, "He had snatched a soul for himself out of a cataclysm," and contrast it with the sentence from the beginning of the story, "His mind was hardly active enough to take a discriminating view of the advantages or perils of treachery."

16. Can you find two striking words in Section IX which might be used as an alternative title for this story?

17. Gaspar's appearance is vividly described in a sentence of 29 words in Section IX. Can you find the sentence?

18. Select from the Scottish doctor's opinion a sentence which forms a kind of précis of the latter part of the story.

19. Note the short and effective description of the upland of Pequeña; another of Peneleo the Indian chief; and a third of Gaspar, "gazing—gazing—gazing."

20. "He could not retreat." Why?

21. There is a slang English word in one of the sayings of Peneleo. Can you discover it?

22. Can you think of any parallel in history or romance to the devotion of Gaspar Ruiz?

23. What do you consider the most touching and human incident in the death scene?

24. Consider the story from the point of view of a drama, selecting the most dramatic incidents.

A NOTE ON JOSEPH CONRAD

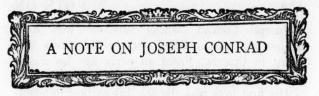

A NOTE ON JOSEPH CONRAD

By Guy N. Pocock

THERE is nothing in all the history of literature more amazing than the coming of Joseph Conrad into the very front rank of English writers, not only for the absolute mastery of a language which he did not begin to learn till he was nineteen, but also for the profound and far-reaching influence he has had and will continue to have on English prose-writing all over the world.

The works of certain writers such as W. H. Hudson and Conrad have been profoundly influenced by the environment of their early years, so much so that it is impossible to dissociate them from that influence. That Keats lived at Hampstead is neither here nor there. One's appreciation of Swinburne is not helped by learning that he had a house at Putney. But that Hudson's boyhood was passed in the Pampas matters very much indeed. That Joseph Conrad spent all his early life at sea in the English Merchant Service matters more than anything else—so much so that before one discusses his writings it is essential to speak of the man's own history.

Joseph Conrad, whose surname was Korzeniowski, was a Pole, and his boyhood was spent in Cracow. From an early age he was a reading boy. "I read, what did I not read!"

His first love was the sea, his earliest determination to become an English seaman. And so in 1877 he joined an English steamer bound for the sea of Azov and England; and before long found himself at Lowestoft. Then he became an Englishman, learning the language which he was to use with such mastery from "sailors of the Norfolk coast, coast men, with steady eyes, mighty limbs and gentle voice."

In 1884 he became Master in the English Merchant Service, for he had never looked back from his life's object, and for ten years lived that sea-life which he has told with a conviction and intensity never surpassed in literature. Then it was that he formed his friendship with John Galsworthy and Edward Garnett, and received from them the encouragement which turned him from sailor to one of the very greatest of English men of letters.

Nineteen years of age before he began to learn the English language! It is a miracle hardly to be believed, yet perhaps in this amazing fact lies half the secret of his style. For every word he used was chosen with the meticulous care of a foreigner, a master indeed of our tongue, but not a native of it. Slowly and painfully, with most earnest concentration, he built up every sentence, giving to the English word a somewhat un-English atmosphere, to be felt rather than explained.

"If you knew," he said, "how much every line has cost me to get out, you would understand my anxiety that none should be lost."

It is this strange atmosphere which is the most striking feature of all Conrad's writing. To read a single page is to enter upon a new plane, a Conrad world, more intense, more ultimately suggestive of the soul of things than the world of experience. The quality of his style is almost magical, with such subtle power and exactitude are the words manipulated. Yet it is not in the unravelling of complexity of motives that his power lies, but rather in the turning of a steady searchlight gaze upon a simple and unchanging mentality, revealing it to us with a clearness that is uncanny.

This constant mentality displays the most complex emotions as the battery of events is brought to bear upon it; and Conrad dissects these emotions with a direct and subtle analysis that leaves us marvelling. But the basic character remains unchanged. Lingard's fidelity in

The Rescue, for instance, remains constant for all his mental suffering and conflict.

For Conrad's characters do not develop. When we first meet them they have already reached maturity of motive, and they do not change. It is his own strong grip of reality and simplicity of insight that make his character-drawing a revelation of truth. Every particular characteristic that he studies implies something universal; and it is not the development of character which he portrays, but the change of situation playing all round and about an unchanging mentality.

To put it in another way: his characters may be likened to Captain McWhirr in his own story, *Typhoon.* Captain McWhirr, a conscious mind, simple, unimaginative, and infinitely steadfast; and all round him, seeking with terrific but unconscious power to overwhelm him utterly, this chaotic turmoil of the typhoon, a blind and elemental fury of hell, and McWhirr, the human intelligence, minute in the midst of it all, carries on triumphantly.

Above all, it is the setting of Conrad's novels which idealises his characters to heroic proportions, like the actors in Greek Tragedy.

The Greek tragedians idealised their characters to more than human greatness. The very actors wore the mask and high tragic shoes to render them unearthly. Conrad loves to portray his characters in a world to us strange and remote—a world of waters gleaming under a tropical sun, or lashed in equatorial frenzy; a world of sun-scorched islands, swamp and heavy vegetation. And there the white men and women, in a strange exotic setting, seem larger than life, more tragic in isolation.

It is not only in the delineation of character that Conrad shows his clear, penetrating vision. In describing places or events he fixes upon essentials with such power and conviction that the scene remains ever after memorable and vivid. Who can forget the sight of that struggling mass of Chinamen sliding, as they fight, with a crash against the cabin-walls of the rolling ship?

One opens a page at random and reads this: "There was nothing for it but to go below with shovels and try to right her, and there we were in that vast hold, gloomy like a cavern, the tallow dips stuck and flickering on the beams, the gale howling above, the ship tossing about like mad on her side; . . . At every tumble of the ship you could see vaguely in the dim light *men falling down with a great flourish of shovels*." It is the truth and exactitude of this last phrase that make the scene in the hold unforgettable.

I open *The Mirror of the Sea* as if taking the

sortes in an old Bible—and these are the first
lines I read: "We saw the crew of the brig from
afar working at the pumps—still pumping on
that wreck, which already had settled so far
down that the gentle, low swell, over which our
boats rose and fell easily without a check to their
speed, welling up almost level with her head-
rails, plucked at the ends of broken gear swinging
desolately under her naked bowsprit." It is *right*
—the very vision of memory is there, as in all
Conrad's descriptions.

It is the Sea—the tropical Sea studded with
Eastern Islands—that forms the main setting of
Conrad's work; not because he especially wanted
to describe the sea, or to bring home to us with
vivid impressionism those unforgettable islands.
It was simply because he knew the sea and the
islands of the East better than anything else;
that he was possessed of a most penetrating
insight and feeling for essentials, and a power of
clothing his perception in words as clear and
convincing as the thing they symbolise. He knew
the sea as a sailor; and he knew it as a poet—
for though he wrote in prose his work is almost
epic. Only two other writers in the language can
approach him in his understanding of the sea—
John Masefield, and Melville, the creator of *Moby
Dick*. Was ever such a night scene, for instance,

as the calm, hot night described in *Lord Jim*—
the pilgrims asleep on deck, and the white wake
stretching out straight as the pencil-line on the
chart? For Conrad knew the sea in all its moods
and significance: he knew its enchantment, its
furies, its "cynical indifference to human suffering and courage," its "irresponsible consciousness of power," and its "unfathomable cruelty."
And not only are his descriptions full of atmosphere and colour more intense and live than
those of any other writer—except at times those
two—but, though a foreigner, he expressed his
amazing insight in the noble rhythmic prose of
perfect English.

And Conrad knew ships. As he himself wrote:
"The love that is given to ships is profoundly
different from the love men feel for every other
work of their hands—the love they bear to their
houses, for instance—because it is untainted by
the pride of possession. The pride of skill, the pride
of responsibility, the pride of endurance there
may be, but otherwise it is a disinterested sentiment. No seaman ever cherished a ship, even
if she belonged to him, merely because of the
profit she put in his pocket. No one, I think, ever
did; for a ship-owner, even of the best, has always
been outside the pale of that sentiment, embracing in a feeling of intimate, equal fellowship the

ship and the man, backing each other against
the implacable, if sometimes dissembled, hostility
of their world of waters."

Conrad's ships are alive—almost sentient. Like
the beautiful women of his novels, they stand with
a noble grace in a far-off setting of tropical seas,
outlandish vegetation, and a few strange Euro-
peans with unfathomable pasts. The perfect lines
of his ships, their delicate response, their bird-
like beauty of motion, all suggest something
more than man-made structures of iron and
wood, something with which these strange,
glorious women alone can be compared.

One more point: it is not the story of his novels
that matters much. One page would tell the plot
of most of them. The basic lines are extremely
simple, however complex that play of emotions
which Conrad handles with such mastery. What
really matters is his marvellously convincing
psychology, subtle to the movement of an eyelid;
strange in atmosphere as a dream that has
come true.

His works are as follows:

1895. *Almayer's Folly :* a story of an Eastern river.
1896. *An Outcast of the Islands :* a novel.
1897. *The Nigger of the Narcissus :* a tale of the fore-
        castle.
1898. *Tales of Unrest.*

1900. *Lord Jim :* a tale.

1901. *The Inheritors :* an extravagant story.

1902. *Youth :* a narrative; and two other stories (*The Heart of Darkness* and *The End of the Tether*).

1903. *Typhoon, and Other Stories.*
Romance : a novel. (Written in conjunction with Ford H. Madox Hueffer.)

1904. *Nostromo :* a tale of the seaboard.

1906. *The Mirror of the Sea :* memories and impressions.

1907. *The Secret Agent :* a simple tale.

1908. *A Personal Record.* (Appeared originally as *Some Reminiscences.*)
A Set of Six : tales.

1911. *Under Western Eyes.*

1912. *'Twixt Land and Sea :* Tales. (*A Smile of Fortune, The Secret Sharer,* and *Freya of the Seven Isles.*)

1913. *Chance :* a tale in two parts.

1915. *Within the Tides :* tales. (*The Planter of Malata, The Partner, The Inn of the Two Witches,* and *Because of the Dollars.*)

1917. *The Shadow Line :* a confession.

1919. *The Arrow of Gold :* a story between two notes.

1920. *The Rescue.*

1921. *Notes on Life and Letters.*

1923. *The Rover.*

Joseph Conrad : a study by Richard Curle ("Studies of Living Writers").

Joseph Conrad : by Hugh S. Walpole ("Writers of the Day").

Wisdom and Beauty from Conrad : selected and arranged by M. Harriet M. Capes.

A uniform edition of the complete works of Joseph Conrad is published by Messrs. J. M. Dent & Sons Ltd., *at* 10s. 6d. *net per volume.*

MADE AT THE

TEMPLE PRESS

LETCHWORTH

GREAT BRITAIN

Margaret MacKinnon
Class III
Portree Sec. School.
Portree,
Skye.

one who doubts
there is God — agnostic
one who does — atheist
not believe in God